Touchdown

PLAYING FOR KEEPS DUET
BOOK TWO

SAMANTHA BARRETT

This is your warning!

If domestic violence, bullying, drug use, date rape and
degrading is a trigger for you then close the book and move
on to another amazing read.
If you are into some dark shit and get off on possessive as
fuck asshole alpha males, turn the page babe and wrap your
heart in a condom because these boys are about to fuck your
feelings, real hard!

Playlist

Fifth Harmony ft Gucci Mane - Down
Piles ft Akon - Hypnotized
Little Mix - Touch
Little Mix - Shout Out To My Ex
Ella Mai Ft Chris Brown - Whatchamacallit
Ella Mai - Boo'd Up
Nelly ft Jeremih - The Fix
Justine Skye Ft Tyga - Collide
Cassie - Me % U
Normani Ft Cardi B - Wilde Side
Cardi B - Up
Vardi B - Bodak Yellow
Sam Smith - Unholy
Jack Harlow - First Class
T-Pain - I'm Sprung
Inayah - Suga Daddy

CHAPTER ONE

Leah

I stand tucked into my brother's side as we watch the exchange between Gary's father and Darius. Instead of looking fearful that one of the richest men in the whole state, shit maybe even the whole country, is standing there promising to ruin his life, Darius just smiles wide looking slightly unhinged.

"Oh, so you only care about *that* son?" Victor's upper lip twitches.

"I'm going to make sure you spend the rest of your life rotting in a jail cell," Mr. Hayes seethes. Gary is on his feet again, thanks to the help of his team mates, clutching his arm to his chest. It brings me great joy to see he is in agony—serves the bastard right. I did as he told me to, okay well maybe I got two out of five off the field but how was I to know only Saint and Darius drink that particular protein shake that I put the powder in! Before the end of the last quarter everyone's phones began to ping with incoming messages. The moment I felt eyes on me I just knew what happened before I even opened the link.

"As long as you're in the one next to me," Darius says like he isn't worried.

"You broke my fucking arm!" Gary screams. Darius just shrugs and smiles at both the Hayes men.

"You're lucky that's all I broke, you rapist." Gasps ring out around us and I drop my gaze in shame.

"That's bullshit and that video proves it!" Mr. Hayes tries to defend his son. Darius steps forward until they are chest to chest. Corvin releases me as he and Beck move in closer ready to pull Darius back if he swings at Gary's dad.

"No, that video just proves that you put your son up to it. You tried to use your golden boy to fuck me over and keep me quiet, except now, it won't work." Victor eyes Darius with careful scrutiny.

"You have no idea who you just fucked with," Victor growls.

"I know exactly who I picked a war with and believe me, I'll fucking win this," Darius spits.

"Someone call the cops, Dad I want his ass arrested," Gary yells like a little bitch. Darius tears his gaze from Victor to look at Gary.

"Fuck," Corvin mumbles, almost like he knows what is about to happen.

"Daddy won't let his son get arrested, he was talking out of his ass. He can't afford the publicity right now with the sale of his company being announced in a few days." Victor's eyes widen, Gary frowns and scoffs.

"I'm not getting arrested, you dumb fuck, you are!" Darius shakes his head and tsks. I look around us to see everyone has stopped and are watching this scene instead of stepping in, I guess this just proves that the five of them really are the kings and no one touches them.

"You didn't hear me, dipshit. Daddy won't let his son go to jail right now."

"I am his son!" Gary screams.

"No, you're one of his sons." I suck in a sharp breath as I look between the three of them with wide eyes.

"What the fuck, Dad, what the fuck is he on about?" Gary demands, but Victor is too busy staring at Darius in shock.

"You picked the wrong twin, Victor. I promise you, I will outshine you and your pick of the litter. When I'm done fucking you over, you won't have two pennies left to scratch together." Gary stares at Darius for a second before snapping his gaze to his father who is grinding his teeth so hard I fear he may snap them. "Watch your back, Hayes, well as best you can because you won't see me coming when I end you." Darius turns and stalks toward me. He doesn't even spare me a glance as he shoulder checks me on his way out. Crue, Beck and Saint shoot me pitying looks before they race after their friend.

I feel sick. Darius and Gary are twins. One raped me and the other one I'm in love with.

Corvin's coach goes to him and whispers something in his ear, Corv nods and marches to me gripping my arm and dragging me from the field. I don't question him when I hear the sounds of sirens in the distance, somebody really did call the cops.

The second we get in the car and Corvin peels out of the lot he starts. "Tell me Gary was full of shit and you haven't been fucking my best friend behind my back for years?" Just as we are about to hit the street, Corv slams on the breaks lurching us both forward but thanks to the seatbelts we both jerk back in our seats. "Fucking hell," he snarls as he winds his window down. I look up and my heart leaps at the sight in front of me. "Either get the fuck in the car or move your asses!" Katie and Cody exchange a quick glace before they both race toward us and climb in the back. I turn in my seat and look to each of them.

They both smile awkwardly and shrug. "We thought you

might need some friends to talk to," Cody says. Too choked up by their show of love for me, I turn around and look over at my brother as he white knuckles the steering wheel and speeds down the road. I frown when he doesn't turn down the street that will lead us to his house.

"Where are we going?" I ask hesitantly.

"Unless the next words out of your mouth are to tell me the truth about you and Darius, shut the hell up Leah." I clamp my mouth closed and slink back into my seat. "Call Beckett." The car's Bluetooth system registers his command and dials Beck's number.

"Where are you?" Beckett says in lieu of a hello.

"About to hit the interstate," Corv answers.

"We got the go bags, I'll get Leah's shit." I frown as I peek over at my brother.

"Pack extra, we got two strays in the back." Cody and Katie bristle at being called strays and I don't blame them.

"Is that a good idea?"

Corvin sighs tiredly, he's dressed in his football uniform, pads and all. "I didn't have a choice, they blocked my car."

"We going off grid?" What the hell does that even mean?

"Yeah, brother, for at least a week until we can get out in front of this shit."

"We'll see you in eight hours." Corvin ends the call.

"Where the hell are we going?" Cody asks.

"To the Batcave." I roll my eyes at Corvin's stupid answer. The longer we drive, the more the ache in my cheek begins to grow. I didn't feel it before but now that the adrenaline has worn off, it's fucking painful.

My eyes sting and my cheek continues to ache but I refuse to say anything and risk Corvin going off at me again. I check the time on the dash and stifle a groan. It's after one in the morning, the girls fell asleep a couple hours ago. If the pain in my face wasn't so bad I would be fast asleep as well. Corvin exits the interstate, I look around and see nothing but mountains. Where the hell are we? We continue to drive for another twenty minutes on darkened roads with no street lights. He finally slows the car and pulls into a gravel driveway that is lined by pine trees. Even with the windows up I can still smell the scent of pine. It reminds me of Christmas. Mom always said we could never have a fake tree, it had to be real or it just wasn't Christmas.

I spot a lone light up ahead and gasp when the car's headlights display the cabin in front of us—it is majestic looking. It's a two-story with a wraparound porch on the second level, and huge A-frame windows, allowing you to see the beautiful mountains that surround the property. Downstairs is all windows, allowing the natural sunlight to beam in daily. Shrubs are planted around the house, and a swing seat hangs on the front porch. Corvin parks the car and shuts the lights off, taking away my source of light. I sigh. I guess I'll just have to take in the beauty of this place tomorrow in the daylight.

"We're here!" Corvin says loud enough to wake the girls. They both yawn and stretch before we pile out of the car. My ass is numb and my back is aching from the long drive, I need a hot shower and some Tylenol to numb the pain in my face, then a nice comfy bed would be great. "Come on," Corv says as he leads the way up the paved path to the cabin. The moon is high in the sky and lights the way for us to not trip on our own feet, well the moon and the porch light. I stumble up the stairs thanks to the lack of lighting. My brother doesn't even offer to help, just grunts and continues to the door. I sigh, Corvin has never been this angry at me before. Katie reaches out and squeezes my hand in silent support. Right now, they are the only two people I have on my side and who actually seem to care about what I went through at the hands of Gary.

Corvin reaches behind the porch light and pulls out a key, he unlocks the door, reaches in and flicks some switches before light blinds us. I blink my eyes to adjust before taking a deep breath and following my brother inside. My jaw hits the floor, this place is stunning. High vaulted ceilings with a chandelier that hangs in the entryway. Beautiful pictures of landscapes adorn the walls, I round the corner and gasp, a sunken living room with high ceilings and another chandelier, white suede couches that wrap around the area and a cozy open fireplace. I turn the other way and find an open plan kitchen with wooden bench tops and a stainless steel gas stove—a pot rack hangs above the butcher's block in the center of the room.

I continue through the kitchen to the open door off the back where Corvin disappeared. I marvel at the room. It's a game room with a pool table, air hockey and a projector screen on the other side with recliners. I follow Corvin as he leaves through another door that leads us past the kitchen and living room. We head up the beautiful wooden stairs that lead up to the second floor. I peek over the side and love how you can see the entire downstairs from the landing.

"That's Beck's room." I turn to where Corvin is pointing to a closed door on the other end of us. "Next to his is… Darius's, then a spare room which your friends can sleep in." I get the double meaning, I'm not to be trusted to share a room next to Darius anymore. "There's the bathroom." He points to the open door next to the spare room. "Then that's my room." He points to the last door, I frown.

"Where do Saint and Crue sleep?" I ask.

"We converted the basement for them, they stay down there," he answers in a clipped tone.

"And, where do I sleep?" I ask as I nibble on my bottom lip nervously. His gaze drills into me and I look away unable to meet his angry glare.

"Next to me so I can make sure you don't sneak out for a

midnight romp." I cringe and Cody snorts next to me. Corvin swings his gaze to her. "Something funny?" he snaps. I expect her to remain silent but she surprises me when she steps into Corvin, spearing him an angry look of her own.

"Yeah, it is, actually. You stand there and judge her for sleeping with your best friend but not once have any of you selfish sons of bitches acknowledged what happened to her! Your sister was fucking date raped and all you care about is Darius fucking her?" She doesn't give him a chance to answer. "You're fucking pathetic and she isn't sleeping in your room either." She reaches back, grips my arm and drags me toward the spare room leaving an open-mouthed Corvin standing there on his own.

CHAPTER TWO

Darius

My forehead is numb from leaning against the window for hours, none of us have spoken a word since we left the house. I know Beck, Saint and Crue are pissed at me. I told them that I wouldn't let things with me and Leah come between any of us and I fucking broke that promise. I'm so fucking livid at her for what she has done to me! But, I'm also so fucking angry at myself for not piecing together what happened to her on my own, I didn't even question it when I found her in that bed, I assumed the worse of her.

"You couldn't have known." I turn to look at Beck, he keeps his eyes on the road as he shrugs. "You aired that shit out loud." I shake my head and go back to looking out the window.

"You know Corvin is gonna beat your ass, right?" Irritated by Saint's stupid ass statement I just flip him off. He scoffs and doesn't take the hint to shut the fuck up. "Stay quiet all you want but you brought this on yourself. You should have fucking told him!" he shouts.

"I know!" I yell. "I should have done a lot of fucking things, but I didn't." My breaths are rushing in and out of me as my annoyance grows.

"Yeah you should have! We are all in the shit because we fucking knew you were fucking his sister and you didn't have the balls to fucking tell him." I fucking hate that Saint is right. I've landed them all in the shit because I didn't come clean. "I won't fucking let this family that we've all created be torn apart. You guys are all I have and sister or not, I won't let pussy come between us." My first reaction is to turn around and punch him in the mouth for speaking about Leah like that. My second, is to feel immense guilt for putting our makeshift family in jeopardy because I fell in love with the wrong girl.

"I'm sorry," I say.

"Not as sorry as Gary is right now," Crue butts in, and within a second the four of us laugh and some of the tension flees from me.

"He's fucking lucky he's still breathing," Beck grits out. I grunt my agreement.

"I really didn't think you were going to drop the twin bomb on him tonight."

"I didn't either, Saint," I answer. I was supposed to save that nugget for the press release on Monday but it just felt like it would cause more damage saying it tonight.

"Hundred bucks says Victor is on the phone to his lawyers now, trying to do damage control." I laugh, Crue is bang on the money. Victor Hayes will be trying to get out in front of the mess I caused tonight, but thing is, he has no power anymore. The reason this merger was so important is because the company we merged with is Victor's. We now own the business that has been in his family for four generations since it was started. Thanks to his gambling problem and shitty investments, we were able to pretty much steal the company out from under him, we just had to make sure he had no idea who was buying it which is why BCD'S didn't buy it per se, we used a shell company to acquire Sullivan Global and all the hotel chains.

"How the fuck are we going to spin you breaking your brothers arm." Hearing Saint refer to Gary as my brother makes my stomach churn. I may share blood with that pussy but he isn't my brother. I have four chosen brothers—well, I hope I still have four.

"Simple, I lost it when I found out my father deserted me and only took my twin instead of the both of us. I was blinded by jealousy that Gary got the life I always wanted while I had to fight to survive because my mother was a junkie and a whore." Saint whistles and shakes his head.

"Fuck me, dude, you're one cold motherfucker but also a genius." I roll my eyes at Saint. We all fall silent. I feel the tension building again and know either Saint or Crue is about to bring the one thing up that I don't want to think about.

"Brother or not, Corvin is going to kill him for what he did to Leah." There it is, Crue just voiced the one thing I was trying to avoid.

"No. If anyone is taking that motherfucker out it's me." My tone is firm and lets them all know I'm not fucking around. Gary won't live to see our twenty-first birthday, I'll make fucking sure of that.

Pulling into the driveway of our cabin, I start to relax. I don't know what it is about this place but being out here in the woods surrounded by nothing but nature always calms me. This cabin was our first big purchase. We wanted something to call our own, a place where we could one day bring our families together and always keep our bond alive. We made a pact, when one of us has a kid, we spend the Christmas holidays here every year no matter what. I see Corvin's car and the tension returns, Beck parks behind him and shuts off the engine. Saint and Crue practically leap out. Beck pops the trunk for them to take all our bags inside while we sit here.

"You have to face him eventually," he says quietly as we watch Saint and Crue lug all the bags inside.

"He's never going to forgive me." A whoosh of air escapes Beck.

"Look, I'm not gonna sugarcoat it for you, okay? Tonight he found out one of his best friends is sleeping with his sister. On top of that, he also just learned said best friend's brother raped his little sister. That is a lot for anybody to fucking digest." Hearing Beck say that shit out loud makes me feel like even more of a piece of shit. I flinch at the thought of those three words. Beck opens his door but before he can get out I grip his arm, halting his escape.

"Don't stop him when he comes at me." Beckett tries to protest but I push on. "He needs this, I've known it's been coming for years, so I'll take it like a man."

"Your funeral, brother," he says as I release my hold on him and get out of the car. I follow Beck up the pathway to the cabin, roll my shoulders and crack my neck side to side, getting myself ready for the beating I'm about to get. The moment I walk through the door I go on high alert expecting Corvin to jump out at me and try to catch me off guard. I keep my wits about me as I follow Beck past the living room and into the kitchen. I freeze at the threshold. Leah stands there with an ice pack against her cheek. I grind my teeth to keep from losing my shit. Saint, Crue and Beckett rally around the lying bitch. She flicks her gaze to me. Her eyes dim as her face morphs into the perfect picture of a guilty person. Unable to stomach the sight of her, I spin on my heels ready to head to my room but instead, I'm met with a fist to the face.

"Fuck!" I snarl as I stumble back a step. I push off the counter and step into Corvin.

"Corvin, stop it!" He and I ignore Leah's plea, his eyes shine with betrayal and guilt courses through me.

"Stay out of this, Leah, and go to your fucking room,"

Corvin grits out between clenched teeth. We stand staring at each other, chest to chest, for a minute not moving a muscle. "Now!" he shouts. A second later, I hear her moving toward us and tense when she brushes past me. Instead of doing as she was told she stops beside us.

"If you want to be mad at someone, be mad at me," she says tiredly. I fight the urge to roll my eyes and step away from her in case some of her toxicity rubs off on me. "None of this is his fault." Corvin turns to face her and I manage to draw in a full breath now that I know we aren't about to fight, yet.

"Let me guess, you managed to convince him to keep fucking you a secret?" he yells. I flinch and she recoils but doesn't back down. She squares her shoulders, lifts her chin and that's when I see the bruising on her face.

Fuck!

I knew Gary was a piece of shit but I didn't think he would fucking punch a woman! The guy is twice her size and from the look of it, she must be in a shit load of fucking pain. I grit my teeth and push those thoughts from my mind. She fucking drugged me, she doesn't deserve my fucking pity!

"It wasn't like that, Corv. If you would just let me explain—"

"Explain what?" he yells, cutting her off. "How you fucking lied to me, Mom and Dad? Or how you lied about why you transferred schools, or what about how you lied about trying to fucking drug us because your fuck buddies twin told you to!" Her bottom lip begins to tremble and her eyes fill with tears. I fucking hate her right now but even I have to admit, Corvin went too far.

"Yes, I did do all of those things," she says as she fights back her tears. Corvin still doesn't budge, he stands there tense and vibrating with anger. "I did it because I didn't want the whole fucking world to see me getting raped!" she screams. Fuck! I turn away unable to look at her, she sounds fucking broken and I can't handle that shit.

CHAPTER THREE

Tears begin to roll down my cheeks, the anger on Corvin's face from a minute ago has vanished. He stands here looking at me like I'm a fragile doll. When his eyes fill with pity, I shake my head so angry at him, at them all.

"I'm fucking sorry. So sorry for what I did, but you have no fucking idea what it's like to have no memory of some asshole defiling your body and yet he has proof and dangles it over your head. I never wanted you to see that or D–" I cut myself off before I can say his name. He keeps his back to me and that stings so bad. "By noon that video will be every-where and everyone at school, shit maybe the fucking world will know what I look like naked and because of who Gary is, no one will believe me, they will all say I wanted it." Darius spins around but I can't look at him, I don't want to see the disgusted look in his eyes. "I thought out of everyone, my own brother would actually give a shit enough to even ask if I was okay, but how fucking stupid was I?" I don't wait for a response. I don't even care if they fight anymore as I make my way back upstairs to the spare room where the only two people who actually care about me sleep.

"Leah." I pause at the top of the landing and don't bother

to turn around. I'm tired and mentally drained, don't even get me started on being emotionally exhausted and wrung out. I hear him climb the stairs but he doesn't stop behind me, he bypasses me to stand in front. Beck's eyes shine with pity, I turn away unable to look at him. "I'm so fucking sorry for what Gary did to you." Hearing that has me slowly turning back to face him, shocked that out of all of them it wasn't my brother or Darius who cared enough to come to me and say that.

When a sob tears from me he rushes forward and wraps his arms around me as I collapse in his arms. He lowers us to the floor as I cling to him. I cringe when the sounds of screams begin to pierce my ears, taking me another second to realize the screams are coming from me. I've never cried like this before, I don't think I have ever really allowed myself to feel the full weight of what actually happened to me that night. There's a pain inside my chest that feels like it's crushing me from the inside out. Beckett tightens his hold on me as he lifts me into his lap. I clutch his shirt in a vice-like grip, terrified he will let me go, not because I'm scared to be on my own but because I feel like I'll fall apart if he lets go.

"Fuck!" The sound of Darius's anguished shout has me burrowing into Beck further as I cry out the injustice that robbed me of my happiness. I may have only found out about this a few months ago, but the truth is, Gary ruined my life years ago when he drugged me and Darius saw what he did. I lost the boy that I loved but I also lost a part of myself that I will never get back because Gary stole that from me.

I hear the others climbing the stairs. I shake my head against Beck's chest conveying to him without words I don't want to talk to them. "Give her to me!" Corvin snaps, I press myself closer against Beck.

"No." Relief washes over me at Beck's answer.

"She's my fucking sister!" Corvin shouts.

"Exactly, Corvin! This should have been you but it isn't

because you and Darius can't pull your fucking heads out of your asses for two seconds and realize it was *her* that was fucked over tonight! She is the one who had her body displayed to the world without consent and I'm the only fucking one who thought to call Troy and have the video shut down and the ball rolling to have Gary charged with child pornography." I tense in his hold unsure what to make of what he is saying, but also grateful that he was willing to do this for me even after he knew what I did. "You selfish sons of bitches both need your faces punched in." His voice drops to an even tone but it holds more weight than if he shouted. "Your sister was drugged and raped, Corvin, and the only thing you cared about was the fact she fell in love with your best friend. You want to be angry at someone, be angry at yourself for not being there for her when she needed you *and* Darius the most."

Beck pushes to his feet. I wrap my arms around his neck and he holds me bride style, then turns and moves toward the end of the hall, where I know his room is.

"I don't fucking think so. She stays with me!" Corvin shouts angrily. Beck pauses but doesn't turn around.

"Do you want to sleep in his room?" he asks me quietly. I shake my head against his chest unable to speak past the sobs that claw their way out of me. "She stays with me!" Beck says. Corvin shouts and rages behind us but then I hear Saint and Crue telling him to chill. They must be holding him back. Beck kicks his door shut behind us and uses his elbow to flick the light switch. He walks us further into the room, then gently begins to lower me but I cling to him. "I'm right here, I'm just putting you on the bed so I can get one of my shirts for you to sleep in." I slowly release my hold on him as he places me on the bed, keeping my chin tucked against my chest lost in my own thoughts.

I cover my face with my hands and cry. The sounds coming from me are foreign and unheard of, I feel so used, dirty and worthless. Seeing that video again broke me, the look on my own face will haunt me forever. The fear and confusion as I stared at the camera has bile rushing up my throat, I leap from the bed ready to race down the hall until Beck wraps an arm around me and ushers me through another door that leads to a bathroom. I race in and drop to my knees in front of the toilet just in time before everything I ate today comes rushing out of me. Beck grips my hair and holds it back as I throw up.

"Get the fuck out!" Beck snaps, I have no idea who's in here and I can't look. I can't stop throwing up.

"She might have a fucking concussion, Beckett!" The sound of his voice has me tensing but I don't look back, I can't as I continue to heave.

"Now you fucking care?" Beck snaps as he brushes a loose strand of hair that slipped free of his hold back. "I got you Lee." I manage to stop myself from heaving and slump back onto my haunches. Beck drops my hair, then turns to the sink as I sit here trying to pull myself together. He returns a second later with a warm washcloth, bends down beside me and gently wipes my face and mouth. I try to smile gratefully but flinch when the pain in my cheek stings—I couldn't feel it while I was breaking apart in his hold, but I can now. "Come on." He chucks the cloth over his shoulder then gently grips my arm and helps me to feet. He wraps an arm around my waist to keep me steady as he turns us toward the door. I tense at the sight of Darius, standing there with a war of emotions on his face. He looks like a dark angel dressed in all black but he isn't an angel and I'm not a saint. I lean into Beck as a wave of dizziness washes over me.

"She can't even stand," Darius grits out. Beck bends down, then scoops me into his arms bride style again.

"Get out of the way," Beck orders, waits a second, before he pushes forward and doesn't give Darius an option but to move. Beck places me on the edge of his bed in a sitting position, grabs the shirt he got for me earlier from the end of the bed, and hands it to me.

"Thank you," I rasp out, my voice is gruff and coarse from all the tears. I can feel how puffy my eyes are already, I'm going to look like a million bucks tomorrow.

"You okay to dress yourself or do you need help?" Beck asks gently.

"Like fuck, you stay the fuck away—"

I cut Darius off, unable to listen to anymore of his fake concern. "It's not like he hasn't seen it all before." That has him clamping his mouth shut. I push to my feet, sway a little and Beck is there gripping my waist to steady me.

"You need help, Lee, you can barely stand." I nod my head accepting that he is right. "Do you want me or… Darius to help you change?"

"I don't care, everyone's already seen me naked so can we just get it over with?"

Truthfully, I'd always choose Darius but I can't stand the thought of his hands on me when I know he can't stand the sight of me. He made it clear he hates me and just thinking that has more tears falling down my cheeks.

CHAPTER FOUR

Darius

Beck reaches for the hem of her shirt and I snap. I shove him out of the way and shoot him a look that promises pain if he pushes this. I may be fucking angry as hell at her and want to ring her fucking neck but I also can't stand here and watch Beck dress her. I grip her shirt, she turns her head away as if she can't stomach the thought of looking at me. Good because I don't want to look at her either, all I see is betrayal. I pull the shirt over her head, leaving her in a pink bra and her pants. I pop the button on her pants and of course it's right at that second the door opens to reveal Corvin, Saint and Crue. Corvin's gaze is laser focused on where my hands currently grip his sister's pants.

The universe fucking hates me today!

"I'm gonna fucking kill you!" he yells as he charges toward me but Beck steps into his path blocking him.

"She has a concussion and just threw up, she can't stand on her own let alone dress herself. Given their history I thought it best he was the one to help her change, I mean unless you want to see your own sister in a thong, then by all means." Beck steps aside, sweeping his arm toward us, taunting Corvin. When Leah stumbles forward into me, I catch her by the waist as she leans her forehead against my shoulder, I shoot Corvin a look.

"Fucking decide, Corvin!" I yell. He takes a look at her, then nods stiffly before turning around. "You two turn the fuck around as well!" I snap. Crue and Saint do as they are told. I make quick work of taking her pants and socks off, reach for the shirt—Beckett's fucking shirt, the thought of her in his clothes grates on my nerves.

"Take the bra off, can't sleep in it," she mumbles.

"Jesus fucking Christ!" Corvin snaps. "I am going to fucking kill you, Darius, but before I end you, I'm going to beat the fucking shit out of you!" I fight the smile that wants to break out at how uncomfortable he sounds. I reach around her and undo her bra, gently pushing the straps down her arms. I ignore the goose bumps that break out across her skin from my touch. I hate that it takes a lot of fucking willpower to not look at her tits, and gently pull the shirt over her head. I help her into the bed and pull the covers up, neither of us will look the other in the eye and I think that's for the best because if we do, I will fucking destroy her for what she did to me. Right now, she is too fragile to handle that. "Now get the hell away from her," he hisses as he shoulders me out of the way to check on his sister. I chance a peek at her, she's already fast asleep, the bruise on her face is fucking dark, her cheek is swollen. "I'm so sorry I wasn't there."

The pain and regret in Corvin's voice spears me. I stalk out of the room unable to be in there any longer. I head straight for my room, needing to be alone so I can sort my thoughts out and to put a plan of revenge into place. The only person who gets to fuck with Leah is me. Gary will get his. I strip off, leaving my clothes on the floor and hop into bed in just my briefs. I can still hear the others next door, that's the one shit part about this place, the walls are paper thin.

"You're not sleeping in here with her!" I roll my eyes, Corvin is being a bitch. Leah is eighteen and old enough to make her own choices. I snort to myself, he's pissed as hell that I was sleeping with her imagine what he would be like if he knew Beck and I both slept with her.

"Get the hell over it, Corvin, and go to fucking bed. Everyone needs to sleep. We'll deal with this shit tomorrow, starting with you and Darius sorting shit." Beckett, always the fixer.

"Fuck him! The bastard betrayed me, he was fucking my sister—"

"Jesus Christ!" Saint snaps. "Are you fucking dumb? They were never just fucking, Corvin. Leah is in love with Darius and whether you like it or not, Darius loves her to." I grind my teeth in frustration, I don't fucking love her.

Liar.

I hate that stupid little voice in my head when it calls me out on my own bullshit.

"Wait a second, how do you know he loves her?" Oh shit, Corvin just figured it out.

"We figured it out a while ago," Crue says hesitantly.

"Man, fuck all of you!" Corvin snaps, then I hear footsteps pounding past my room. A door slams a moment later, Corvin is big fucking mad!

"Well, that went well," Saint says, chuckling lightly. "We're going to get some shut eye, dude. Need anything before we go?"

"I'm good, I'll catch you in the morning." I'm on edge the second I hear Beckett's bedroom door close and Saint and Crue head to bed. I last two minutes before I'm leaping out of my bed and throwing my door open. I stop and glare at the smirking fucker leaning against the wall outside my room. "I wondered how long it would take you."

"Fuck you, you touch her–"

"And you'll do what, D? You made it clear tonight that she is dead to you and you want nothing to do with her." He's right, I do fucking hate her but that doesn't mean I'm ever going to be okay with seeing her with anyone else. "I'm fucking beat and need a solid eight hours of sleep and I can't get that with you glaring holes through my wall." I stare at him confused until the fucker barges past me into *my* room, closes the door and locks it. "Go to bed, Darius," he calls from the other side of the closed door.

"You locked me out of my room!" I seethe.

"I sleep naked, would you rather me sleep next to Leah with my cock out?" The laughter in his tone pisses me off. He thinks this is a joke but none of this is funny to me. I stalk back to Beck's room and close the door. I stand here and stare at her sleeping form in the soft glow of the bedside light. How can someone so evil look innocent? Too tired to deal with this shit I decide to just get this night over with. I slip in on the other side of her and make sure there is plenty of space between our bodies.

"What the fuck!" I bolt upright in bed still groggy from sleep. I look around confused for a second until it all comes rushing back to me—the game, the video, coming to the cabin and Beck locking me out of my room which means, I drop my gaze to my side to see Leah still sleeping then turn back to the doorway where Corvin stands seething. "Get the fuck away from her!" he snaps. I oblige without complaint, wanting to get as far away from her as I can. I throw the covers back ready to climb out of bed but her voice has me stilling.

"Both of you go the hell away!" It's not the anger in her voice that has me tensing, it's the fact she thinks she has the right to be pissed at *me* after what *she* did! I feel her shifting from me and peer over my shoulder to watch her climb out of bed. She stands there with her hair wild and untamed, her eyes are red and swollen from all the tears last night. I slowly climb to my feet and stare her down—I hate the sight of Beck-ett's shirt on her.

"You're going back to Mom and Dad's today." Leah's eyes widen for a second before she schools her features and nods.

"Fine. I'm also dropping out of school and moving." That has both me and Corvin stumped for a second but he manages to gather himself quicker than me.

"Fuck no! I just paid your tuition so your ass is staying in school!" I scrub a hand down my face as I shake my head. He just let the cat out of the bag and Leah is smart enough to have caught his little slip up. She places her hands on her hips and cocks her head to the side.

"*You* paid for my tuition?" Corv darts his gaze briefly to me before focusing back on the she devil.

"Yes! Now, shower and meet me downstairs." He chucks the bag I didn't notice he was carrying at her. She catches it, then shoots him a glare before rummaging through her bag to grab some clothes. The moment she grabs out a black bra and matching lace thong, I know I'm dead when a gasp sounds from the doorway. That was the thong he had twirling around his finger not long ago in my room asking if he knew the girl it belonged to.

"You son a bitch!" he roars before he flies across the room, a fist landing to the right underside of my jaw, a left hook connecting with my ribs before another right hook has me falling back onto the bed. Leah screams for help and for her brother to stop but I can see the look in his brown eyes. If I fight back, it will destroy any hope I have of ever repairing the damage I have done to our friendship. "Fight back, you fucking pussy!" He leaps on top of me and swings a good fucking right hook that has my head snapping to the side. I see the guys in the doorway, Beck fighting to hold Saint and Crue back from interfering and stopping Corvin. "You fucking bastard," Corvin screams as he lands a hit to my ribs.

I groan in pain. "You took advantage of my sister." He rears his arm back, ready to hit me again.

"I was the one who came onto him!" His arm freezes midair as he looks at Leah. "We were at Tyresse's party and you said I wasn't allowed to drink, but I did anyway. Darius found me and took me home. I kissed him that night and told him…" I close my eyes and brace myself for the torment that her words are about to put me through. "I told him I loved him."

Corvin snorts. "It doesn't matter what you did, Leah, he took advantage—"

"Fucking hell, Corvin, while you were away with Mom and Dad at football camp, I walked into his room, stark naked." Corvin cringes in disgust. "He told me to get out. I refused and do you really want to know the rest?" Corvin rests back on my thighs as he looks between the two of us.

"How long?" he asks in an even tone with his gaze on me.

I don't pretend to not know what he is asking. I hold his gaze as I answer. "Pretty much the whole of senior year," I answer. his chin drops to his chest and I feel like a real dick for not coming clean.

"Who else knew?" he asks in a dejected tone.

"No one, Beck only figured it out when Leah moved in and Saint and Crue only know because they overheard us fighting. They never betrayed you, the three of them warned me to stay away and I… didn't." Corvin slowly lifts his gaze to me and I hate that I can see he doesn't trust me.

"She's the reason you pulled away from me and closed me out, isn't she?"

"Yes," I answer honestly. I ignore Leah's sharp intake of breath.

He nods like he can finally understand why I put so much distance between us. "When this is all over, you will stay away from my sister."

"Corvin–" He ignores Leah and continues on.

"You'll pack your shit and move to Chicago and run the daily operations of BCD'S from there, you won't call or ever come back." His words feel like he dropped a boulder directly on top of my chest, the air sucked from my lungs. I knew when the truth did come out that he would be pissed but I didn't expect him to banish me from his life entirely. My worst fear is coming to life, I'm going to be alone again but this time, I won't have either Williams' sibling by my side.

CHAPTER FIVE

Leah

I sit on the couch next to Cody, with Saint on my other side. No one has said two words since Corvin told Darius he had to leave. The guys tried to change his mind but Corvin wouldn't budge and what could they really say when Darius agreed to my brother's terms. On top of everything that I am already feeling, I can now add feeling like a homewrecker to the list. I never meant to come between my brother and Darius. I knew he would be angry but I never thought he would throw away years of friendship with D because of me!

"Take these, it will help with the pain." I flick my gaze up to see Crue standing there with a glass of water and two pills in his hand. I eye them skeptically for a moment. "It's just pain relief for your cheek." I take them and the water from his hands, mumbling my thanks before handing the empty glass back to him and flopping back against the couch. Cody rests her head on my shoulder, I lean my head against hers, sighing. Beck and Corvin disappeared to organize some press release thing that I have no idea what for. Darius has been locked in his room all morning while the rest of us hung out downstairs.

"Holy shit!" I snap my gaze across to the other side of the

room where Katie sits on the window love seat with her phone in her hand. I frown, how the hell does she get service here? Katie flicks her gaze to Saint and Crue who are both already staring at her with curious looks on their faces. "Gary just released a statement saying that Darius paid him to sleep with Leah and he was the one who drugged her!" Crue and Saint are across the room, peering over Katie's shoulder reading whatever it is she is showing them.

"Fuck!" Saint curses. "Beckett, Corvin, Darius get the fuck in here now!" he shouts. It takes a second before I hear feet pounding the stairs and then another two sets coming from the theater room end of the cabin.

"What?" Corvin snaps. Saint turns to face the three newcomers with a grave look on his face. I peer over the back of the couch to see Corvin and Darius have kept a couple feet of space between them, not wanting to be near each other. It kills me that I can't go to him and wrap my arms around him, promising that he isn't alone. That I'm right here by his side, but there is so much water under the bridge that I can't get past my own hurt feelings.

"There's a warrant out for Darius's arrest for breaking Gary's arm. The Hayes are pressing charges against him and you're wanted for questioning as well." My stomach sinks.

"Fuck, we need to call Troy," Beck grits out.

"Wait, how the fuck do you know that?" Darius asks cautiously. Saint and Crue both step aside to reveal a smug looking Katie who slowly climbs to her feet, takes a deep breath and squares her shoulders as she stands between the guys.

"I found it," she says confidently and a little bit smug.

"How? There is no cell service out here and Corvin had a blocker put in place to stop anyone from tracking us while we are here." Katie doesn't cower under the accusation of Darius's words like I assumed she would. Cody and I both shift so we are looking at them all over the back of the couch.

"I feel like this is the best time to tell you all something you don't know about me." The five guys tense. "I am a dancer and I love what I do, but my true passion is in computer science. I'm really good at it, which is why I was able to nullify the blocker you have. I was also able to reroute your Wi-Fi that you have disabled and have it re connected so I could get online." Saint and Crue stare at Katie with their mouths opened in shock. Beck, Corv and Darius look stunned. Katie drops her gaze and scuffs her foot along the wooden floorboards.

"You're the one who hacked into Beckett's computer, aren't you?" Katie looks up at Saint nibbling her bottom lip, she nods. I stare at her in shock. I look to Cody who seems just as shocked as the rest of us that our friend slash room-mate was able to keep something like this a secret from us!

"Look," she says as she runs her gaze over each of us. "I know your lawyer is good and all but he sucks at computers and is slow as shit. I had the video scrubbed from the web two minutes after I got in Corvin's car. If anyone sends the link to try to keep it circulating their phone is going to download a virus and wipe their entire phone including the cloud."

"Why the secrecy?" Darius asks as he steps forward eyeing my friend warily.

Katie snorts. "Dude, guys don't like it when a chick is smarter than them or able to hold her own. Imagine me being able to tell them on a date that I know what their SAT scores were?" Darius doesn't look convinced. Corvin steps up beside him and I'll admit I'm more shocked that he didn't keep an ocean of space between them. They may be mad at each other but when shit hits the fan, they will always band together. I see that now.

"What did you find on Beck's laptop?" Corvin asks her, his tone is filled with warning. Katie gnaws on her bottom lip nervously. Crue turns to her, reaches out and uses his thumb to pry it free. Her eyes shoot wide as she stares up at him, her cheeks tinge red.

"You gonna answer my friend, doll?" he says in the sexiest voice that has me waiting with bated breath to see what happens next between them.

"Uh… I… um." Katie shakes her head causing Crue to drop his hand back to his side. "I found contracts and files on there about the Hayes." All five guys turn ridged.

"What else?" Saint asks as he steps into her back, plastering himself flush against her, drawing a gasp from my poor friend who is now sandwiched between him and Crue.

"I know this merger with Sullivan global goes public in two days. I also know you have been trying to find dirt on Saint's dad's company." I see Saint stiffen behind Katie at the mention of his dad. "I didn't find anything at first but the moment Gary released the video and I tracked the IP that granted him web wide access it led me back to Saint's father's company and this video isn't the first he has released to gain him the upper hand."

"What does that mean?" Saint grits out. Katie turns so her back is now to Crue as she faces Saint. She reaches out and places her dainty little hand on his chest.

"Your father uses his company to help blackmail other companies into selling their stocks, assets and many other things because of the back door access he has to their servers. I'm sorry Saint, but your father isn't a good man and he has been trying to find dirt on you and your friends since the contract for Sullivan Global was drafted. I put a firewall in Beck's computer to stop it from being hacked again but he can access your phones and other devices you have that are connected to the internet." My jaw is practically on the floor, not just from the information Katie is sprouting but from the sexual tension that is pulsing between Saint, Crue and Katie.

"How much do you know about what we are doing and why we are doing it?" Darius asks. Katie flicks her gaze to him and then me for a split second before focusing back on Darius.

"From what I could gather off of Beck's laptop, you have had this ball rolling for about four years. I must say, what the five of you have accomplished in that short amount of time is freaking impressive, men twice your age couldn't do half of what you five have done." Corvin and the others puff their chests out with pride. I hate that I'm still confused as hell as to what is going on here. "Except, with the merger going public in two days, you are going to have to do damage control and if I may suggest, you and Darius call your lawyer and discuss the charges so it doesn't look like the youngest billionaires in the United States ran from the police." I choke on my own spit.

"Say what now?" I squeak out as I stare directly at my brother. Corvin doesn't even spare me a glance as he answers.

"Guess you were too busy sleeping with my best friend to notice I was the one paying all the bills at home." I recoil at his harsh tone. I drop my gaze in shame. "You're gonna help us," he demands. Katie shakes her head. "You don't have a choice, you either help us or I have *you* arrested for hacking." I balk at my brother, he is being a complete dick right now.

"Fine, but you all have to sit down and explain to Leah what you have done. She has a right to know that Gary only targeted her because of what you five planned to do to his–excuse me, and Darius's father." I flinch at the reminder of Darius and Gary being twins. My stomach churns just thinking about it. Corvin reluctantly agrees. The guys come round and claim seats on the couches, Beck taking the spot next to Corvin and shoots Darius a smirk. It's then that I realize the only available seat left in the room is beside me. Sighing, I say,

"Just sit down, Darius, don't be a douchebag." He spins around and pins me with a look loaded with disgust. I keep the hurt from my face.

"You're one to talk, Goldie. Sitting there acting all innocent and shit when it's your fault all of this has happened." I climb to my feet pissed off that he would dare stand there and blame me for any of this.

"My fault?" I shout. "How the fuck is it my fault *your* brother drugged and raped me, huh?" He closes the space between us until his chest brushes against me, forcing me to crane my head back to meet his stare.

"I told you to stay home!" he growls.

"I only went because I didn't want you to be on your own when you told Corvin," I snap right back.

"Tell me what?" Corvin asks in an icy tone. Darius slams his eyes closed, I step around him and face my brother.

"Darius planned to tell you about him and me that night. I didn't want him to have to face your wrath on his own, so I snuck out to meet you all at the party, then Gary…" I clamp my mouth shut and drop my gaze to the floor. I try as hard as I can to fight back the tears. It seems that's all I do these days is fucking cry. I'm so over crying! Darius grunts as he is shoved aside by Beck, arms wrap around me pulling me against him. I return his embrace without thought.

"I promise you, sweetheart, Gary Hayes will not get away with this. I swear." Call me crazy but I believe Beck.

CHAPTER SIX

Darius

I have to bite the inside of my cheek to stop myself from snapping at Beck to get the fuck away from her. How can he forgive her so easily after what she did—tried to do to them but only succeeded in getting me and Saint benched. She could have done anything else and I would have forgiven her but not when it concerns drugs. I refuse to end up like my crack whore of a mother.

"Can you tell us what Gary did or said to get you to…" Beck lets his sentence trail off so she has a chance to back out if she doesn't want to answer. She nods. They break apart and sit down leaving the only seat vacant next to Corvin. I grit my teeth and drop down beside him, ignoring how he flinches when my leg brushes his. Beck wraps an arm around her shoulders and pulls her into his side. Cody reaches over and places her hand on the top of Leah's thigh offering her resilient support.

"I was waiting for Darius and you guys to arrive when Gary came to me and offered me a drink." Her tone is flat and void of emotion as she speaks. "I refused the first time, I didn't want Corvin to catch me drinking and piss him off before we could tell him about… us." Corvin is grinding his teeth so hard I can hear it. "But as time dragged on and none of you guys showed up, my nerves got the better of me. When he offered me a drink again, I took it and downed the whole thing." She chokes up and tries to take some deep breaths to calm herself enough to continue, I'm two seconds away from fleeing the room not wanting to hear any of this. "I just remember feeling dizzy and then…" She slowly lifts her gaze to mine and the duplicity in her gaze has me stiffening. I feel Corv burning holes into the side of my head but I'm trapped in the orbit of her green eyes as they hold me captive. "Calling out for *you.*" Tears flow faster down her cheeks, my breathing becomes unsteady. "I kept crying out for you, I couldn't move, I didn't even know what was happening."

"I thought you couldn't remember?" Beck asks tentatively. She nods and smiles sadly but never takes her eyes off me.

"I couldn't. It wasn't until Gary showed me the video that memories of that night came flooding back. I don't remember all of it but I do remember him carrying me upstairs and telling him I was waiting for Darius. He laughed." I clench my hands into fists, her eyes beg me to not look away or she'll lose the nerve to continue, so I don't. I hold her gaze the whole time offering her my strength. "He said *'by the time I'm through with you he won't want you again. Breaking you will break him.'* I didn't know what that meant but I knew it wasn't good. I screamed for you!" she growls, the venom in which she says it tells me she blames me for not being there sooner and right now, I blame myself as well. "I woke up feeling sick and confused. I didn't understand what happened or why I was naked but there was…" This time she drops her gaze, I brace myself for her next words to send me free falling over the edge. "So much blood, I never bled when… Darius and I had sex." Corvin groans and scraps a hand down his face.

"What happened next?" Beck gently asks.

"I got changed, walked home expecting to find Darius in his room and ask him why he left me at the party. At that time

I thought I had spent the night with him but then I couldn't find him anywhere he just... vanished. Blocked my number and I didn't see him until the following year at Thanksgiving." My eyes narrow at the memory.

"Why the fuck did you bring Gary to thanksgiving then?" Corv grits out.

"I saw him in town when Mom and I went to get the plum sauce. He stopped me out the front of the store and made small talk, then said he was alone as his dad was away. *I didn't invite him, Mom did!* You know what she's like. She never wants anyone to be alone during the holidays, neither of you two gave me a chance to explain. As soon as dinner was done you both took off and I haven't seen you until I transferred."

"You transferred because of him." It's not a question but she nods anyway so I push on. "Did he tell you to drug us before or after you transferred?" She blows out a breath before speaking.

"After. I was still at DCU when he showed me the video. I heard him bragging to a couple of his friends as I was walking past. I stopped when I heard him mention my name. He proceeded to tell his buddies that he ruined Darius and made sure he would never look at me again. I hit him up and he showed me the video. I went into a dark hole. I dropped out of dance and school unable to stomach the thought of ever seeing him again knowing that he had... been inside me." She chokes out a sob, I'm fucking powerless to stop myself. I'm out of my seat in the next second crossing the room, smack Beck's hand away from her and lift her into my arms. She wraps her legs around my waist, wraps her arms around my neck and buries her face in the crook of my neck as she cries. "I'm so sorry," she sobs.

I push all my anger away as I stand here holding her, not giving a fuck that her brother is behind me. Right now she needs me. "None of this is your fault," I say quietly. Beck stands and offers me his seat, I take it with her still in my hold. I meet Corvin's stare over her shoulder. I don't see any of the anger from earlier—his eyes brim with tears as he watches his sister break down and tell her story. Last night none of what she said registered because we were both too angry and caught up in our own shit to process the fact that Leah was hurt by Gary because of *us*.

"I-I never meant to hurt you." She hiccups. I rub my hand up and down her back trying to soothe her.

"Don't worry about it, Goldie," I say. She pulls back and stares down at me with doubt in her eyes.

"I don't know how he found out I was transferring to CHU but he did and started calling me, texting me and telling me if I didn't take you five out of the game, he was going to post the video. I… I couldn't let that video get out. I didn't want you to ever see it." Her face contorts in pain as she cups my face with her hands. "I never wanted you to look at me like I was ruined. I was so scared to come to you or Corvin."

"Why?" Corvin demands. She doesn't take her eyes off me as she answers.

"I was scared neither of you would believe me. Gary told me no one would ever believe me if I went to the police. He said his father would make sure that everyone knew I was the one who wanted it. I never wanted it, Darius, you have to believe me." She cries harder, I shift forward and grip her face between my hands and swipe her tears away with my thumbs.

"I would never have doubted you for a single second, Goldie." My words seem to ease some of the tension in her body.

"I'm going to fucking kill that motherfucker!" Corvin announces. I grunt my agreement and so do the others. Her green eyes shine with an emotion a lot like hope, but if I'm being honest with myself, I don't know if I'm ready to pick up what she's putting down in regard to where we stand.

"We can have him done with the distribution of child pornography and link it back to Saint's father." I peer around Leah to stare at Katie. This girl is a fucking mystery, and by the looks of things, she has gained the attention of both Saint and Crue without even trying.

"How?" Beck asks.

"If I'm calculating things right, Leah was underage and Gary wasn't so we can counter the arrest and charges. As far as Corvin and Darius go with the beating doled out to Gary, Corvin was enraged his sister was hurt and Darius was protecting his girlfriend." I tense at the word *girlfriend*, Leah doesn't miss it.

"How do we do this?" Crue asks, again Katie cuts in.

"Simple, you lay low until the press release tomorrow and explain that no one ran. You both decided to take Leah out of town so she could rest and get help to overcome the tragedy that she went through. You then apologize for your actions and accept any charges thrown at you." The guys begin to protest but she raises her hand halting them. "Hear me out. If you both accept responsibility for your part and explain why you did it, no one is going to side with Gary. The press is going to eat him alive when you announce that your girl-friend slash sister was targeted by the Hayes family because of you being successful without using your rightful name, and them wanting to destroy you by using Leah to do that." I mull over her words for a moment. What she says does ring true but it's a fucking risk.

"If they do this, that means we all have to go public and announce that we are the owners of BCD'S which means everyone at CHU will also know we own the school." Leah and Cody gasp, Crue frowns at them but continues. "You know there is a chance that the school board will vote us out of school, right?"

"Our football career will be over," Saint whispers.

"No, it won't," I say as I lift Leah off my lap and place her on the seat beside me. "Victor is bluffing. At the press release I'm going to announce he is my father and my twin brother found out, in his rage he targeted my ex-girlfriend." I feel Leah bristle next to me. "I'll tell them that I snapped and had a mental breakdown, given the circumstances and my positions at CHU, I'll announce I'm dropping out and… moving to Alaska to run our resort." Everyone begins to shout and throw in their piece of how we should do things and I appreciate their efforts but they know this is the only way we can get out on top. If I stay, Victor will find a way to come after us and I can't allow them to take the heat for me.

"What if I come forward and charge Gary?" Leah says quietly. She may have muttered the words but we all heard them loud and clear.

"You don't have to do that," Corvin says.

"If I do it, will it help?" she asks her brother. He cuts a glance at me. I nod, letting him know if Leah does this then it would take some of the heat off us and allow us to continue on the path we have paved.

"Yes, it would," he says in an even tone.

"Okay, I'll do it," she says with conviction that has me feeling proud of her.

CHAPTER SEVEN

Leah

We spent a couple of hours sitting there listening to how my brother and the others began their company and amassed their fortune through the stock market. I'm in awe of how they managed to accomplish all of this while in school and playing football. Proud of the sheer determination they all had to make sure they never struggled to want for anything. I learned Saint hates his family and wants nothing to do with them. Crue only has his aunt who brought him up after his parents abandoned him when he was one. Darius, well everyone knows he has no one except us so it made sense for him to push for this to excel. Corvin, I get it. He has always wanted to make sure our parents were able to retire and never worry about money again—his reasons are noble. Beckett is a closed book, the guys don't even know his whole story and it baffles me why he won't confide in anyone about his past. After that, the guys disappeared to get everything in place for tomorrow. Cody and Katie wanted to practice our routine but I wasn't feeling it. So, I decided to hide out on the balcony of the second floor and stare out at the mountains.

"Can I join you?" I look to the side to see my brother

standing there with his hands stuffed in his pant pockets, a remorseful look on his face. It's getting dark now, which means I must have been out here for hours and not known.

"Depends," I say.

"On?"

"Are you going to yell at me again?" His shoulders hunch forward as he shakes his head. "Then sure, you can." He makes his way over to me and drops down into the seat beside me as we stare at the amazing view. We remain silent for a long time lost in our own thoughts until Corvin finally breaks it.

"Why my best friend, Leah?"

"Why not him?" I retort.

"Because he's my best friend and you being with him complicates that." He runs a hand through his hair and slumps back in his chair. "I trusted him with you. He betrayed that trust Leah. I'll never allow you and him to be anything, I can't." I swivel in my seat to face him.

"That isn't your call to make. Darius is a good guy—"

"He was the fucking one who found you in bed with Gary and left you there! Why the fuck are you sitting here defending him?" He's angry and I get it, but I won't allow him to blame Darius for what happened to me.

"What happened with Gary wasn't his fault. He told me not to go to that party, I didn't listen so that is on me, Corv, not Darius."

"Leah, you're eighteen. You have so much time to do whatever you want before you settle down with a good guy who treats you right." I bristle at his dig.

"Darius is a good guy!" I defend. He lulls his head to the side and pins me with a pitying look.

"You need to let him go, Leah."

My stomach sinks. "Why should I?"

"Because he will never forgive you for drugging him." My

breath hitches. "Darius swore he would *never* touch a single drug and risk becoming like his mother. He never hooked up with any girl who dabbled in any type of that shit. He barely drinks because he's worried he'll become an addict. You doing what you did to not only him but Saint as well, is unforgivable to him, Leah."

"I'm sorry. I'll tell your coach it was me and not them–"

"You don't get it!" he says with his voice raised. "It's out of coach's hands now, it's with the board. On matters that concern each of us we aren't allowed to vote. They are going to be kicked off the team. Darius will be pissed but he'll get over it. But, Saint, he won't. Unlike Darius and Beck, me, Saint and Crue planned to go pro and if Saint is out, then Crue won't go without him. Your actions have cost us all, Leah. You could have come to me and I would have helped you deal with this but you didn't trust me enough!" I bite the inside of my cheek to focus on something else aside from the pain I feel inside my chest. "You slept with him and fucked with his emotions. What the hell did you think would happen when all of this came out?"

I open my mouth, then snap it closed. I truthfully don't know what I thought was going to happen. "I thought I would figure a way out of it, then Gary showed up at the diner that night and I knew I didn't have a choice," I whisper in a defeated tone.

"Darius broke his arm. He will never play again and despite what they all think, I know Victor Hayes, he is not just going to let Darius off the hook for that one." I flinch.

"What does that mean?" I press.

"It means, tomorrow isn't going to go our way no matter what we do. The press has their story and they don't care about the truth. They just want drama and the headlines don't paint you in a good light, sister." I balk at him.

"What do you mean?" I ask hesitantly.

"They are saying you have been sleeping with the twins the whole time and that what happened yesterday was your fault." I splutter, that is not true. I never even knew about them being related!

"Corvin, I—" He holds his hand up silencing me.

"It doesn't matter what you, me or anyone else thinks or knows. Ninety percent of the world believes what they read. We'll try to do as much damage control as we can but I can't promise this won't blow back on you."

"I get it," I say in a dejected tone. "I'm going to be the whore who bagged DCU's best QB and the girl who fucked her brother's best friend." Corvin flinches but doesn't say anything, which makes me believe that is exactly what people are going to be saying about me.

We all sit around the twelve seater dining table not saying a word. I push the food around my plate. I'm not even hungry, the thought of food makes me nauseous. Plus, chewing hurts thanks to fucking Gary's fist. Beck filed a police report pressing charges against Gary for hitting me and started the process with their lawyer to have him charged with rape. Beck said I would have to give a statement and tell the police what I told them today. I wish I could just put this whole ordeal behind me, but that can't happen until after tomorrow. The guys are leaving early tomorrow morning to head into the city, the girls and I are staying back at the cabin.

"I'm out, thanks for dinner Beck," Darius says as he pushes back from the table, loads his plate in the dishwasher and heads upstairs, not sparing me a glance once. Corvin is right, Darius is never going to forgive me for what I did to him and honestly, I can't blame for that. I just wish his dismissal of me didn't hurt as much as it does.

"Ya'll need to talk or something because the tension is killing me!" I ignore Saint, I don't need any of them weighing in on my situation with Darius.

"Shut the fuck up, there is nothing to sort," Corvin snaps, the tension in the room only amplifies, thanks to his outburst.

Laying here on the couch, I can't stop from tossing and turning. Cody and Katie offered to share a bed so I could have the other but I refused. They have been put through enough thanks to me, so I refused to allow them to be any more uncomfortable then they are already by being locked away in this cabin for a week. Corvin glared as I carried my pillow and blanket downstairs, but I just ignored him. I know it is going to take a long time for him to trust me again.

"He'll forgive you." The sound of Darius's voice has me bolting upright and turning toward the kitchen where he leans against the wall sipping a glass of water. My eyes drink him in. Thanks to the soft glow of the moon I can make out that he is only in a pair of sweats. I fight the groan that wants to break free.

"How did you know that?" I ask to distract myself from ogling his body.

"You talk out loud."

"Hm," is my only response. I don't know what else to say, saying sorry won't fix what I did to him.

"I'm gonna break this down for you, Goldie." I sit up straighter in my seat and watch as he saunters into the sunken living room with a swagger only he can pull off. Rather than sitting on one of the seats he drops down onto the coffee table directly in front of me. I dart my tongue out to wet my lips, his eyes track my every movement causing me to flush red. "I may not be able to see it but I know you're blushing." I snort and quickly clamp my mouth closed. He releases a tired sigh and I slump into the couch.

"Just say whatever it is," I hedge.

"Fine. You and I are done, for good." Getting a white hot branding iron to my heart would have hurt less then hearing those words come from him. "You crossed a line, Leah, and there is no way for you to come back from that. Even when I thought you cheated on me, I still gave you a second chance!" The hurt that laces each of his words feels like a knife to my heart. "What you did… I can't get over that and I'll never forgive you for it. So, from here on out, you stay away from me and I stay away from you. Don't text or call, better yet, just delete my number." I nod stiffly. "Look, I'm fucking sorry for what happened with Gary and I swear I'll do everything in my power to make him pay. If you had told me, things would have been different but instead you lied and used us."

"I did try to come to you. I called, text and searched for you but *you* left! Who the hell was I supposed to turn to?"

"Your brother," he snaps.

"How the hell was I supposed to explain what happened to Corvin when he had no idea about you and me? Would you have rather I outed you and told my brother that we were together?"

He shakes his head, climbs to his feet and stares down at me with a vacant look in his eyes. "You did the damage, now you live with the fall out of the choices you made." He storms out without another word leaving me alone to deal with this on my own. I know he's right and I did fuck up, but can he not for one second see it from my side? I can't let this go. I race after him, catching him just as he's about to close his door and shove it open. He stumbles back in shock before pinning me with a glare. "Get out!" he snarls.

I ignore him as I push his door closed and move toward him. "You stand here judging me because I made a mistake, a mistake I will forever regret, halfback. I won't keep saying sorry. You want to hate me go for it, but just know the feeling is mutual because *you* left me without a word. You could have come to me and you didn't, you ran like a pussy!" That pushes him over the edge, he gets right in my face breathing heavy.

"Get the fuck out, Leah. I told you we're done. You want to go spread your legs for the fucking team and let them run a train? Do it because I don't fucking care anymore!" he screams. I stare at him in a new light. He's hurt and I get that, but it doesn't mean I have to take his shit.

"Fine. Remember you said that shit, because I'm tired of waiting for you to man the hell up and admit to my brother you're in love with me." He scoffs then laughs darkly.

"Aww, Goldie, your sweet and innocent act may fool everyone else but not me. You are a lying little cunt who likes to play games. Well, guess what, baby," he reaches out and tucks a stray strand of hair gently behind my ear, which shocks the hell out of me, "I'm going to ruin you for taking the only family I have ever known from me. I'm going to fuck your world right up and relish in seeing you burn in front of my eyes." My mouth drops open in horror. How the hell can he be so cruel, when hours ago he held me while I broke down in front of everyone. The door opens. Darius flicks his gaze toward it and rolls his eyes. "Get the fuck out. Your bodyguard is here to save you from me."

"You're being a fucking dick!" Beck snaps. Darius turns his dark eyes back to me. I don't find any trace of the kind attentive lover anywhere in the depths.

"And still she wants me. Fancy that, Becky boy. The girl you're pining over still wants my cock in her even when I'm a cunt but not yours. That must be a huge blow for the ego." I gasp as his hurtful words, shaking my head in disgust.

"Fuck you, Darius, you are a real piece of shit–"

"Don't fucking call me what you call my brother!" he seethes.

"Then maybe you shouldn't act exactly like him!" I shout before spinning around and storming toward Beck. He steps aside to let me out. I don't fuck around, I head downstairs even though I know I won't be able to sleep a wink after that confrontation.

CHAPTER EIGHT

Darius

The second we walk into the hotel lobby where the press release is being held, cameras are shoved in our faces. Troy calls out to us and tries to fight his way through the paps. We manage to push our way through the cameras and follow after Troy as he leads us into a room off to the side. Beck has to force the door closed and lock it so no one can barge in.

"Fucking hell, that was intense," Crue says as he drops down into one of the vacant chairs around the oval-shaped table.

"We only have twenty minutes before we have to head in, take a seat," Troy says, the rest of us grab a seat and wait for him to stop shuffling through the files he has and tell us what the fuck to do. "Okay," he says as he grabs a stack of papers out. "I received a call last night from Victor's lawyers."

"About?" Saint butts in.

"They wanted to renegotiate the terms of the contract given the events that unfolded on Friday. I said no and that the press release would still go ahead today."

"They're coming, aren't they?"

"Yes, Corvin, they are already waiting for the conference

to begin." When we all start shouting Troy raises his hand to silence us. "We can come out on top of this."

"How?" I snap. "I broke his fucking arm and beat the shit out of him. Our stocks are going to drop the moment we go public as the owners of BCD'S."

"They are going to bury us in legal shit and halt all the plans for us to expand the hotel chain," Crue interjects.

"We're fucked," Beck breaths out as he leans back in his chair.

"Boys!" Troy snaps, gaining all our attention. He smiles cunningly as he slaps his hands atop the table and looks to each of us. "I must admit, I thought you were all finished but then this morning I got another call."

"From who?" Corvin asks.

"A witness," he answers.

I frown. "A witness to what exactly?" I ask.

"Gary Hayes telling Victor Hayes that he *did* in fact drug and rape Leah. It was all caught on camera and the witness is here to speak today." I dart my gaze to the guys to see they are just as shocked as I am.

"How does this help us?" Saint asks.

"It would mean that the charges Gary has pressed against Corvin and Darius won't hold much weight now that there is proof their attack was warranted in the defense of Leah Williams. All we need to do is have both Corvin and Darius make a formal apology before anything is mentioned about the merger. When the merger is announced, Darius will then close out the conference by saying he is heading straight to the local precinct and will be out on bail within a couple hours." A whoosh of air escapes me.

"I'll still have to go to court though?" I ask.

"Not if I have anything to do with it. Now, let's get this over with and get the hell out of here because I have a mountain of paperwork to finish and new employee contracts to draft for you boys."

"And this is why we keep you on retainer, Troy," Crue jokes, earning a scowl from the old man.

I stand from my seat and look out at the crowd of reporters, spotting Gary and Victor in the back with smirks on their faces. It brings me great fucking joy to see Gary sporting a cast on his throwing arm. I fucking hate that I have to say sorry to the son of a bitch and act like I mean it. Troy said I have to sell it or I risk fucking up this whole thing up.

"Ladies and gentlemen, firstly we would like to thank you all for being here today. Before we dive into the announcement I would like to address a matter that occurred Friday night at Crestview Heights University involving myself, Corvin and another player from DCU–"

"Is this about the fight?" someone yells. I nod.

"What was the cause of the fight?" a woman shouts.

I recite the speech Troy had told me to. "An explicit video was shared by Gary Hayes involving Corvin's underage sister. Gary drugged and raped her."

"Allegedly!" is shouted from the back. I focus on Gary allowing a small smirk to be seen on my face as I speak.

"No. This is the truth and we have proof." Gary turns to his father who is glaring directly at me.

"Mr. Lockhart, is the rumor true that Gary Hayes is in fact your brother?" I plaster a fake smile on my face and answer the guys question. We have always been in the spotlight because of how well we play football, but recently, since rumors spread that we may be the owners of one of the wealthiest stock companies in the US, the press have been sniffing around a lot more lately.

"It is." Murmurs break out around the room. "Gary is my twin brother and Victor is my father. We were reunited when Victor graciously sold his company to us."

"What company?"

"Who bought it?"

Questions are shouted but I ignore them as I press on. "I apologize for my outlandish actions on Friday night. I know because of the severity of it that I will be barred from taking the field again. But I don't want my actions to overshadow the real reason we are standing here in our newly acquired hotel." If looks could kill, I would be dead and six feet under from the way Victor is looking at me. More gasps ring out and questions are shouted at me. Corvin stands beside me turning the attention to him. He raises his hand and a hush falls over the room, waiting to hear what he has to say next.

"I would also like to extend my sincerest apology to you all for my actions. I have no excuse, except that seeing my sister being hurt and abused by that man sent me spiraling into a fit of rage, which I am not proud of." He points directly at Gary who looks utterly thrown by the turn of events. "My sister was nothing but a means for him to use to get at me and… Darius."

"Why would that affect Mr. Lockhart, your sister being hurt?" A guy calls from the front. I stand beside Corvin wanting to answer for him. Troy warned us someone would ask this question and it had to come from Corvin, not me to show we have no bad blood. But that's a lie, Corvin won't even look at me.

"Because at the time of the… incident, my sister and Darius were dating." Before any more questions can be asked, Corvin raises his voice to be heard over them. "We will be pressing charges against Mr. Hayes and my sister will also be pressing charges for assault as he punched her in the face." Angry shouts erupt as cameras are turned away from us for a moment to snap pictures of Gary and Victor as security leads them from the room as questions are being shouted at them about the *incident*.

"If I could redirect all your attention back to the front,

please," Troy calls. "Thank you, now for the actual reason we are all here. I would like to introduce you all the new owners of Sullivan Global, soon to be known as Saint Hart Holdings. As you may all have deduced by now, these five young men are the founders and CFO's of BCD'S, the most profitable stock trading company in the US. These five young men have applied themselves to this business and sunk every cent they had into making sure it excelled and it did. BCD'S will remain as a stock trading company but with the merger of Saint Hart Holdings, the resorts will run as they always have, as will the hotels, but they will also now offer master classes in stock trading. What these five young men have achieved at the tender age of twenty is incredible. Now, are there any questions?"

We have question after question hurled at us for at least an hour before Troy finally calls it. I'm beyond grateful to get the fuck out of here and take off this monkey suit he made us all wear. I don't do a suit and tie, never have and never will. We're ushered straight outside into a waiting limousine that will take us to the police station downtown.

"You boys did great. You all handled yourself well and dealt with Victor and Gary with poise. Now, I must say, I don't think we have seen the last of them." I grunt out my agreement, too nervous to speak. There is so much that could go wrong with me handing myself in like this. There is no guarantee that I will be granted bail and I refuse to spend the next few years in a cell.

By the time we finish at the station, it's dark out. I'm fucking hungry and pissed off that I've been sitting in a cell for hours. The only reason I was let go Troy said is because Gary dropped the charges against me. Why though? We stand around the empty car park at the back of the station waiting for Troy to get off the phone to whoever the hell it is.

He ends the call then looks to Corvin before looking at me. "Gary dropped the charges because apparently he received a call from a young woman who threatened—excuse me—warned him that she would come forward and press charges for blackmail, rape, assault and a few other things. Gary had no choice but to withdraw the charges or spend the better part of his life behind bars." Surprise courses through me. I look over at Corvin to see he has the same look on his face.

"How did she call when there is no signal at the cabin?" Saint states.

"Clever girls," Beck whispers.

"What does that mean?" Crus asks.

"We took Corvin's car and they clearly took mine into town." That was… actually really smart, but something tells me Beckett left his keys in a place they could find them because he knew Leah wouldn't be able to sit back and do nothing.

"Look, boys, we still need to do a few more press releases now that you five have come out as the owners. You have a Forbes 500 company now. You boys own hotels, resorts and shares in two colleges, you have amassed an empire and I'm proud of you all. But, your work is just beginning, so be ready for the press to be following your every move. Don't do anything dumb." We all agree to Troy's terms and promise to be on our best behavior. The limo takes us back to the hotel so we can get Corvin's car and start the eight hour drive back to the cabin. We're all quiet and lost in our own thoughts as Corv drives us back. It's hard to believe that four years ago this was a pipe dream. We all busted our asses and put every penny we had into investing. The truth is, we were lucky that one of the investments we made took off and allowed us to bring in more income so we could grow quicker than we ever thought.

"My dad is gonna know about this," Saint whispers quietly from the back.

"He can't do shit. Troy has already started the process of taking him down. Once that has begun we'll partition his board and go in for a hostel takeover and push his ass out. The board will be put to a vote and trust me, Saint, they are gonna want you to run that shit." Corvin is right, the plan was to always take Victor out and then go after Saint's dad.

"I know. It's just fucking hard, ya know. I mean, we know he has been dealing in shady shit involving distributing videos of kids but to actually see his work in action with that video of Leah…" He lets his sentence trail off. We all feel the same. This is a lot for anyone to take in.

"You guys know what this means, right?" Crue asks from his seat in the middle of Beck and Saint.

"What does it mean?" Corvin asks tiredly.

"We don't have to hide any more and watch what we spend so no one suspects us. With Victor out of the picture and shit being public, Devon is gonna know he's next." I see Saint deflate out of the corner of my eye at the mention of his father and I feel for him. He didn't always hate his father, but when we brought him the evidence of what his father was really doing, he couldn't deny it. He jumped on board with our plan straight away and hasn't looked back since. His loyalty is awe inspiring but we also know this is fucking hard for him.

CHAPTER NINE

Leah

I spot Corvin's headlights through the windows, my nerves go haywire inside me knowing that I probably overstepped and pissed him off more. I thought going to the police would be the right thing, at the time it seemed like a really good idea to do it but now as I sit here in the living room, with my friends on either side of me, I begin to doubt my decision. When the headlights cut off, I take a deep breath and begin to pick at my hangnail. I wish I had trained for another hour with the girls, maybe then I would have been too tired to care. When the sound of car doors close, I begin to pick at my nail harder.

Cody places a hand on top of mine, shooting me an encouraging smile. "We're right here with you, every step of the way."

I melt a little inside. "I don't know what I did to deserve you both but I am so grateful to have met you," I say to them both. We share a quick awkward three-way hug just as the front door opens, then we slowly pull apart. I sit here biting my bottom lip as I slowly lift my gaze to see the guys walking in. I release the breath I didn't know I was holding at the sight of Darius.

He's safe.

He glances at me for a brief second before he turns and heads up the stairs, Cody grips my hand and squeezes while Katie leans her head on my shoulder. Saint and Crue wave out as they head for the basement to have an early night. Beck and Corv drop into the couch opposite us, both looking wrecked. Corvin rests his head back on the couch as he gazes up at the vaulted ceiling.

"I see my car is still in one piece." I cringe and shoot Beck a toothy smile that has him smiling back.

"I swear I didn't scratch it and I even put gas in it." He narrows his eyes at me.

"Leah, I don't give a shit about you using my car. I knew your ass wouldn't be able to stay here and do nothing, so I left the keys out on the counter." That shocks me. I cock my head to the side and study Beck. He may be quiet but he pays attention and listens to everything. It's weird to find a guy who actually does that.

"You saved his ass, you know." I pull my gaze back to Corvin who still won't look at me.

"What do you mean?" I ask hesitantly.

"You going to the cops saved his ass. He would probably still be sitting in a cell right now if it wasn't for you." I flinch at the casual way he says that, like it isn't a big deal that his best friend could have gone to jail because of me! I climb to my feet, glaring at my brother. The girls follow my lead. He lazily lifts his head and looks at me with a bored expression on his face.

"You can be angry all you want but guess what, Corvin, none of this has anything to do with you." He opens his mouth but I push on needing to get this out while I have the nerve. "You're just angry because Darius and I went behind your back. Look how you're acting now. This is the reason we never wanted to tell you because we knew you would act like a damn baby! Grow the hell up and get over it. I'm eighteen and will do whatever the hell I like. Starting tomorrow, the girls and I are going back to school and if you don't like that then you can suck a dick!" I storm out of the room with my head held high, but on the inside I'm screaming because I can't believe I just said that to my brother! I race up the stairs and slam to a halt when I spot Darius leaning over the banister as I reach the landing. He turns his head toward me with a ghost of a smile on his lips. The girls slip past me and head for our room, closing the door quietly.

His eyes spark with mischief as he looks at me. "Corvin can suck a dick, huh?" I snort out a laugh and quickly cover my mouth with my hand and nod. He nods a couple times before he pushes off the banister and moves toward me. My breath hitches when he stops a step away from me. His brown eyes bore into mine, his hair flops forward onto his forehead and I want to reach up and push it back, but I don't. "Thank you for what you did today, you didn't have to."

"Yes, I did," I say quietly, afraid that any loud sound will scare him away.

He shakes his head as a sad smile graces his handsome face. "Nah, you didn't. Enjoy school, Leah, and I hope you and Corvin sort everything out." He tries to walk away but I reach out and grab his arm pulling him to a stop. I stare up at him in fright, panic begins to claw its way up my throat.

"Why did that feel like a goodbye?" I ask, scared that he may actually leave.

"Because it was. I finished what I set out to do." I shake my head rapidly.

"You can't go, you… you can't leave. You have to stay!" My voice rises as hysteria begins to take hold of me.

"Corvin needs space—"

Before he can finish he's cut off. "You run away like a pussy, then don't fucking come back. Be a man and face this shit." I spin around to face my brother and stumble. Darius grips my waist to steady me. Corvin's gaze is laser focused on where his best friend's hands are now gripping me. Darius drops his hold on me and steps back. "That shit," Corvin says as he points between us. "Doesn't happen. Leah, you're moving back to the dorms when we get back. You stay the hell away from Darius. If you don't, his face is going to pay the price." My mouth drops open in shock, I expect Darius to rebuke his claims but he just stands there silently. "Go to bed, Leah. We're all leaving early tomorrow morning to head back." His tone is final. I shoot him a glare before I shoulder past Darius, angry that he didn't say anything and just stood there like a mute. I slam the door closed to my room only to find my friends sitting up in their beds with shit eating grins on their faces.

"We have a plan," Cody says excitedly.

"Operation make him regret letting you go is in operation," Katie says before her and Cody break out into giggles. Whatever their plan is, I'm in!

We've been back at school for two weeks now since leaving the cabin. I barely see any of the guys except for Beck. I know Saint is still mad at me and I honestly don't blame him but when are they going to let this go? I mean for God's sake, they are back on the team. Once they explained everything to their coach and what happened, they were reinstated but I didn't get off as lucky. I was lucky not to be kicked out and I think I have my brother to thank for that, but I was kicked off the dance team and that fucking sucks! Mrs. Telford said I can try out for the team again next year as long as there are no more incidents. She accused me of drugging Kyle and the others, but I truthfully had nothing to do with that. I'm still being monitored by all the staff and all the students here hate me because of what I did to their star players. Most of the students still make lewd remarks about the video—those comments are harder to ignore than I would like to admit.

"Heads up." Katie says from her seat next to me on the picnic table. I look up to see Garrett and a couple of other guys making their way over to us. Aside from Cody and Katie, Garrett is like the only other person who will speak to me in public. I knew people would be pissed but I didn't expect to be the social outcast. I feel like Moses, everyone parts when I walk through the halls.

"Hey, beautiful," Garrett says to me when he reaches us. Cody gags earning a glare from Garrett, Katie blatantly ignores him—neither of the girls trust Garrett. They think he is using my social outcast status to his gain, thinking that I will change my mind and give him a shot. I'm still not even close to thinking about another guy or dating. I've been texting Darius every day since we got back. For the first few days he would leave me on read but now he just won't even open my messages.

"Hey," I reply.

"So what are your plans tonight?" he asks, and I shrug.

"Nothing, movie night I guess."

He tsks me. "Nope. You ladies are coming out with us tonight." I frown and shake my head.

"I don't think that's a good idea—"

"Nonsense!" he says while smiling down at me.

I sigh. "Garrett, I appreciate the offer but no one here wants me at any parties and I don't feel like getting yelled at or mocked by more girls." The guys around here just act like I don't exist, but the girls go out of their way to make sure I know that I am hated and the worst of them all is Chelsea. She likes to throw it in my face that Darius is so over me and blowing up her DM's.

"Well, lucky for you this isn't a party. A friend of mine from back home is the DJ at the local club and I happen to know the bouncer so I can get you ladies in." I look to Cody and Katie who both shoot me looks saying *hell no*. "Come on, I know you must want to dance and let loose. We have a bye game this week, so no one from school will be there, they will be at Shayla's party." I won't lie, the thought of dancing and being able to hang out without having to worry about being glared at does sound appealing.

Fuck it.

"YOLO," I say smiling up at him.

He grins down at me. "Sweet, I'll pick you ladies up at ten out front of your dorm." I nod and wave as he and his friends head to practice.

"You're playing with fire, Leah." I turn to Katie who is shaking her head.

"How? I can't stay locked in that dorm room for another night. I can't even go anywhere without being harassed. I need this, please say you'll both come," I beg. I can't even practice in the gym or on the quad without being abused and our dorm room is too small for me to dance in. Cody and Katie trade a loaded look before Katie throws her head back and groans. I squeal and clap like an idiot. For the first time in weeks I actually feel excited.

CHAPTER TEN

Darius

"Yo!" Saint shouts loud enough to be heard over the pounding bass of the music that plays at Shayla's. He shoves his phone in my face and I frown at the picture of Leah, Cody and Katie all dolled up and wearing scraps of clothing that don't leave much to the imagination, the caption reads.

L_Wills_<3 - YOLO, girls night out on the town, let's dance bish's.

I flick my gaze back to Saint as I hand his phone back to him. He shakes his head, clearly annoyed I'm not picking up what he's putting down.

"Read the fucking comments!" I grab the phone from him again and scroll through the comments. It pisses me off when I see guys commenting on how hot she looks but the one comment that stands out to me has me clenching Saint's phone so tight, I may actually break it.

G-Bizz_69 - See you in 10, gawjus, can't w8 to see you move.

I snap my gaze back to Saint. "Where the fuck are they going?" I snap.

"I asked Dylan, he said Garrett mentioned going to Smart Bar because his buddy is the DJ."

Fuck! I scour the crowd trying to find Corvin. I spot him

on the couch with a brunette sitting on his lap. I storm over to him and tell the girl to beat it. She pouts but does as she's told. Corvin drunkenly climbs to his feet trying to scowl at me.

"What the fuck?" he growls right in my face.

"We have to go, your sister is at a club." He scrunches his face in annoyance and waves me off as he drops back into his seat and motions for the girl to come back. "Corvin!" I yell, pissed off he isn't listening.

"You go, you seem to know more about my sister than I do, so you go and save her ass." I grind my teeth in anger as I grit out.

"Garrett took her to a club." Within a second the girl is pushed off his lap and he is on his feet. His eyes are clear now as he looks at me.

"Get the others, we're leaving." I smile and nod as I rush off to find Beck and Crue.

⚜

We managed to find a parking spot a block away. When we get closer, we notice that there is a line half way around the block of people trying to get in. We bypass the line and move straight to the front. The bouncer opens his mouth to tell us to fuck off I'm sure, but I pull out five hundred from my pocket and wave it in his face. He snatches it and opens the red rope for us. People shout and curse us out but we ignore them, money talks and it will gain you entry to anywhere. The second we push through the main doors, the bass of the music hits me, Akon's "Hypnotized" blares thorough the sound system. The place is packed.

"How the hell are we going to find her?" Corvin shouts in my ear. I'm about to say we need to split up when the crowd begins to part as the music begins to quiet down and the DJ speaks.

"I got a surprise for y'all. I need y'all to back up and make some room for my girls, Leah, Cody and Katie to do their thang for y'all." Before he has even finished speaking the five of us are pushing our way through the crowd to get to the center where the patrons have formed a circle to watch the show the girls are about to put on. The moment the DJ blasts Fifth Harmony's –"Work from Home" the crowd on the other side opens to let the girls through.

Fuck me!

Leah looks… like a fucking wet dream. Her hair is straight and out, she wears this tiny little black top where the sleeves are off her shoulders, only big enough to cover her tits. She's wearing denim cut-offs that are so fucking tiny they only just cover her pussy and expose half her ass cheeks. But it's not the clothes that have my cock getting hard, it's the knee-high black come-fuck-me boots that she's wearing. Images of me fucking her in those boots race through my mind—my cock is rock fucking hard now.

"Jesus Christ!" Corv snaps. I look over to him expecting to be focused on his sister. I follow his gaze and my eyes widen in surprise to find he is focused on Cody and not Leah. Cody is dressed in a one-piece purple outfit that has a split from the top to her bellybutton. When they twirl around and bend over all their asses are on full display for all to see. Guys go nuts when they start to thrust their hips and throw their heads back as they run their hands down their body.

"Get it, Katie baby!" Saint shouts from behind me. I peer over my shoulder to find him and Crue both jumping up and down cheering and hollering for Katie. What the fuck is going on with them and the computer geek? I turn back to the girls when the crowd screams louder. I scowl as Leah and the other two lay flat on the floor and begin to pound their fists against the ground as they push their asses up and down like they are fucking. Having had enough of the fucking free porn show she's putting on, I take a step forward but Beck slaps a hand against my chest halting me.

"What the fuck?" I snap.

"She needs to win this, D." I frown confused at what the fuck he is saying until he points across from us and I see Chelsea and two other girls I recognize from Leah's old dance team. Fuck me! They're having a dance battle! I'm proven right when the song ends and the three girls slink back into the crowd as the others take the floor. None of them have the sex appeal or the stage presence like Leah. They move to Little Mix's "Touch" but nothing about the way they move makes me feel anything. To be honest, I have secondhand embarrassment for them. The crowd seems to love it when they all begin to dance all over each other.

"We gonna stop this or what?" I snap, but then zone out when I see Garrett push his way through the crowd and hug Leah from behind. I clench my fists at my side, she looks tense and uncomfortable in his hold.

Tell him to fuck off, Goldie.

It brings a satisfied smirk to my face when I watch her untangle his arms from around her waist, then plasters a fake smile on her face as she turns to talk to him. I hate that I don't know what she is saying. My blood begins to boil when he bends and whispers something in her ear that has her throwing her head back and laughing. It's in that moment Cody turns toward us and her eyes widen. I shake my head and place my index finger against my lips urging her to not say anything. She darts her gaze back to Leah then back to me—no, not me— she looks at Corvin who stands next to me stiff and brimming with anger. I dart my gaze between the two of them, trying to get a read on what the hell is going on between them, but my attention is snagged when the song ends and the DJ speaks.

"Dammmmm, y'all! I can't choose, I think we need a final round." The crowd goes crazy. "I got y'all, how about for the final round we make it interesting." The crowd goes nuts beginning to shout out their suggestions. "Okay, I like that one. What do ladies say to a lap dance?" I turn ridged, grinding my teeth so fucking hard I think I may actually break them. I feel eyes on me and I look to my left to see Chelsea grinning at me as she shouts her agreement. I turn back to Leah and the girls to see them deep in conversation then they nod and Leah steps forward.

"Fuck this!" Corvin snaps, but Beck cuts in before he can end this.

"You storm out there and drag her out, she is never going to make it at CHU. She has to prove herself and winning this will do that." Corvin glares at Beck, his face is turning red with anger.

"I'm not watching her give some douchebag a lap dance!" he grits out.

"Ladies pick your men!" The DJ calls. I spy Chelsea stalking toward me and I know I have a choice to make, I swallow my nerves and turn to Corv pleading with my eyes that he sees I am the better option. "Hell no!" he snaps angrily.

"Corvin, Chelsea is coming to get me to throw her off. Let me do this for *her*." He searches my gaze for a minute. I begin to worry that he is going to deny me and I know seeing Chelsea with me will throw her off her game, making her lose.

"Don't fucking touch her and this doesn't change shit!" I can tell that was painful for him. I nod my agreement just as Chelsea reaches us.

"Come on, good-looking." I allow her to take my hand and lead me out to the center of the dance floor where there are now two chairs waiting. I cut my gaze across the crowd to see Leah standing there with wide eyes, her brows push in, as hurt begins to show on her face. Garrett slides in beside her and leads her out to where I stand with Chelsea. She drops her gaze to the floor unable to look at me.

"What's wrong, Leah? You seem… upset?" Chelsea taunts. Leah shakes her head and slowly lifts her gaze to peer up at me through her lashes.

"I… I can't watch this–" The DJ announces for us to take a seat. Chelsea pushes me down into mine as Garrett slip-drops into his with a shit eating grin on his face as he looks at the beautiful blonde standing in front of him. I know I said I would ruin her but I can't, not with how hurt she looks right now thinking she is about to watch Chelsea grind all over me. I flick my gaze to Corvin who looks like he is ready to throw hands and mouth. *I'm sorry.* If this is what she wants then Leah is gonna have to woman up and come get me. I know she can do it, she just needs to come claim what's hers.

CHAPTER ELEVEN

Leah

I can't look at him.

It hurts too much knowing that Chelsea is about to give the best performance of her life and using *my* man to do it. I shoot Garrett a look ready to tell him that I'm sorry I can't do this, but then the DJ drops the beat and *our* song comes on. I spy Chelsea begin to move out of the corner of my eye and I don't know what it is that comes over me but when Ella Mai begins to sing, a possessive urge to claim him comes over me. Without thinking I dart across the floor until I'm standing directly in front of Darius, his eyes blaze at the sight of me. Chelsea begins to protest behind me but everything begins to fade away except for the music, me and him. I place my hands on the tops of his knees and push them open before slowly dropping down in front of him and then popping my ass out as I slowly rise up.

"We have a switch up, folks!" The DJ shouts. I sweep my leg out wide as I spin around and face Chelsea, then reach behind me and place my hands back on his knees as I hold her gaze and slowly lower to the floor right in front of him, but this time, I go down into a side split. The crowd goes wild. Her eyes blaze with hatred as she scurries over to

Garrett to try to salvage this battle. I push up to my feet and take a couple steps away from him before spinning around to face him. I bend my knees and run my hands all over my body as I sway my hips before dropping to my hands and knees. I flick my hair round and round, before thrusting my hips up and down as I slide across the floor, right in front of him. His eyes burn with lust as I grip the tops of his knees and stand right between them. He sits up straighter as I run my hand through his hair, then grip the back before pushing his face forward until it's in line with my pussy.

"Damn, my girl Leah isn't playing," I hear Rex the DJ call out over the mic. I release my hold on his head, then push him back as I spin around and drop down onto his lap, grinding my ass against his… holy shit! Darius is hard as fuck. I continue to swirl my hips as I lean back against his chest and rest my head beside his. Our eyes lock as I reach for his hands and run them all over my body. His eyes burn with raw need and fuck, I'm a slave to that look.

"Move for me, Goldie." Those four words light a fire in my belly as I push off him and spin around so I'm straddling his lap. I grab his hands and place them on my ass—the crowd goes off. I place my hands on his shoulders as I lean forward and begin to bounce up and down on his dick for a few seconds before I smack his hands away and mimic *Jordan's* move that she did to *Chris Brown* and recline back until my hands are on the floor and flip back into a front split right in front of him. He leans down until our faces are a sliver apart. I lean forward and ghost my lips over his just as the song ends. The crowd goes crazy but we stay frozen in this position staring into each other's eyes, my breaths coming out in rapid pants. "Leah–" He's cut off when hands grip my hips and I'm hoisted into the air. I spin around and come face to face with Garrett.

"You fucking nailed that!" he shouts excitedly. I smile my thanks and turn back to Darius, my shoulders hunching forward as I fill with disappointment when I see the chair is now vacant. Cody and Katie are there in the next second screaming in my face.

"We won!"

"You killed it," they shout in unison. I smile and join in on their excitement, deciding to unpack what just happened when I get home to my dorm room. The crowd surrounds us and shouts their approval. The DJ begins to play again and everyone starts to dance but this time, I'm not really feeling it. My mind is too focused on the fact that Darius was here and I gave him a fucking lap dance. I feel my cheeks heat with the memory of feeling how hard he was beneath me. We spend the next hour dancing and having fun. Garrett doesn't seem bothered at all by the fact that I ditched him in front of every-one, and gave Darius the best lap dance of his life–well, I hope it was.

Garrett leads us out of the club with his buddies following behind. They are actually pretty cool guys and so easy to talk to. Nathan is gay and such a freaking vibe, the guy is amaz-ing! I told him I planned to make him my new BFF. He agreed and put his number in my phone. As we all stumble outside, Cody and Katie bust out laughing at something Nathan said.

"I mean it, I would have licked that man like a fucking lollipop!" I smile and quirk a brow at Katie, she rolls her eyes playfully and says.

"Nathan wants to lick Darius like a lollipop." My brows jump into my hairline as I stare at my new BFF.

"Baby cakes, he is too much man for little old you." I snort and shake my head.

"Who cares about Lockhart. Him and his friends are a bunch of dicks." I bristle and pin Garrett with a disapproving look.

"Those *dicks* you are referring to are *my* friends as well and one of them is also my brother! I would appreciate it if you would stop making snide remarks about them," I say in a stern tone. I yelp when an arm wraps around my waist and pulls me back flush against a rock-hard chest. I relax immediately when he rests his chin on top of my head, I don't need to see him to know who it is. The way my body hums to life just from his nearness tells me who it is.

"Yeah. Garrett, stop making snide remarks," Darius mocks. I'm too flustered by the feeling of him pressed against me to chastise him for being rude to Garrett. The latter stands there scowling at Darius, his face is a mask of fury.

"You're like a leech. Why don't you and your band of misfits bugger off, we have plans." I search my brain for a memory of us making plans and come up blank. We had all agreed to call it a night, so I don't know what plans Garrett is referring to.

"A leech she doesn't mind sucking on her." I gasp as my eyes shoot wide.

"God dammit, I knew that was more than a dance," Nathan whines, causing me to laugh. Darius pulls back but keeps his hands on my waist. I look around to find it's only him and Beck here. "Baby cakes, you ever had two men at once?" I choke on my own spit as I hear Beck and Darius cough behind me, trying to mask their laughter. Nathan darts his gaze to the two guys behind me, and when understanding dawns in his eyes, I quickly cut in before he can out my secret to the group.

"Well, I'm beat and going to call it a night," I announce, forcing a yawn out.

"Dorms are locked, it's after curfew so you ladies can crash at our house," Garrett kindly offers. I smile my thanks.

"Nice try, Garrett boy, but they're coming home with us." Garrett's eyes burn with hatred as he stares at Darius. Honestly, I would rather crash at my brother's house than in a house filled with strange guys that I don't know. To stop this from getting out of hand, I pull out of Darius's hold and give Garrett a quick hug and thank him for tonight before I turn to my new BFF, who wraps me in a bear hug.

"Baby cakes, I want all the details, every single one over coffee tomorrow," he whispers. I giggle as I pull back and shoot him a wink. Nathan darts his gaze over my head, he has zero shame as he checks Darius and Beck out. He whistles between his teeth then lets out a dramatic sigh. "I bet they both have huge ass cocks and know how to use them." I splutter, so do Cody and Katie.

"Right, so on that note, deuces," Darius calls out as he grips my hand, and yanks me toward him. He drags me across the road with Beck and the girls following us.

"Scream my name when you come riding his juicy cock, baby girl!" Laughter bursts out of me. I hear the girls laughing hysterically behind us as well at Nathan's remark.

"You need new friends," Darius grumbles as we reach Beck's car. I slip into the backseat with the girls as Beck slips behind the wheel and Darius rides shotgun.

"Oh my God, I love Nathan!" Cody giggles beside me.

"Babes, same!" Katie agrees.

"Hey, he's mine!" I cut in causing the three of us to break out in another round of laughter. The laughter dies in my throat when Darius leans around his seat and pins me with an angry look.

"Who the fuck is Nathan?" he growls.

Cody snorts. "The guy who wants your cock in his ass." Katie and I break out into uncontrollable laughter at Cody's answer. The horrified look on Darius's face is priceless.

"How much have you three had to drink?" The three of us girls share a look before laughing again. "Leah?" Darius snaps.

"We may have had a few or is it a couple, maybe I don't know. Nathan kept bringing us fruity yummy drinks," I answer, which just earns me another look from the broody bastard. "Stop looking at me like that. You're just pissy because I made new friends and you weren't invited tonight. Wait, why were you there tonight?" Rather than answering he turns around and faces forward but I'm not having it. Maybe it is the alcohol but I feel reckless and emboldened suddenly. I climb over the console, ignoring Darius's shouts to sit my ass down. Beck swerves but rights the car.

"Leah, sit the fuck down!" Darius yells. I manage to climb in the front and plant my ass right on his lap, then unclick his seatbelt while he sits there stiff as a board. I pull the belt around both our bodies and clip it back in as I shimmy back against him. I feel his cock twitch in his pants and smirk triumphantly.

"Now that you can't escape me, tell me why you were there tonight. Don't lie either because Cody told me she saw you with Corv, Saint and Crue as well." It takes him a minute to finally relax back into his chair. When he does, he wraps his arms around my waist and pulls me flush against his chest. I rest my head on his shoulder. Suddenly feeling really sleepy, my lids begin to grow heavy, and I feel myself drifting off to sleep.

"Because I didn't want you to choose Garrett." I swear I hear him whisper before sleep claims me.

CHAPTER TWELVE

Darius

Beck kills the engine when we pull into our drive. Saint's jeep is here so they must be home. Corvin refused to hang around the club and wanted to go back to the party. I refused to leave, which pissed him off more. Beck drove the three of them back to get Saint's car before coming back to get me and the girls. We sit here for a moment saying nothing. Beck checks his rearview mirror and sighs.

"They crashed as well?" I ask.

"Yeah, you want to take her in and I'll take Katie then come back for Cody?"

"Yeah," I say tiredly. I unclip my belt ready to get out when Beck's words stop me.

"She needs to go in the spare room." It grates on my nerves that he's telling me what to do with her but I also know he is right.

'Yeah, I know," I answer somberly. I push the door open and maneuver Leah so she is laying bride style in my arms. I carefully climb out of the car, making sure she doesn't hit her head, then turn to see Beck lifting Katie from the car, holding her the same way I hold Leah. We both make our way toward the house, Beck comes to a stop in front of me at the porch steps. I peer around him to see Corv sitting there. He looks to me then drops his gaze to his sister in my arms. He sighs as he runs a hand through his hair.

"Cody in the car?"

"Yeah, she's out cold," I answer, taken back that he isn't yelling at me for holding his sister. He even seems like he's sobered up. Did they even go back to the party?

"You two take them up, I'll get Cody," he says as he climbs to his feet and steps around us to head back to the car. Beck shoots me a look. I just shrug and shake my head.

"Let's go before he comes back and yells at me," I say, causing us both to chuckle quietly as we make our way inside. We pass the living room and come to a stop at the sight of Saint and Crue sitting on the couches watching a movie. "I thought you guys would still be out," I say. They both look over the back of the sofa and the second they spot Katie in Beckett's arms they are launching off the couch and rushing around to grab her off him. Utterly baffled and weirded out at the sight of Crue holding the girl close to his chest, with Saint running fingers down her cheek tentatively, I decide to leave them and their fucking trio issue alone, then head upstairs.

I climb the stairs and head for the spare room. The door is ajar so I use my shoulder to push it open. I walk over to the bed and gently lay her down before reaching for the throw blanket at the foot of the bed. I pause at the sight of her boots. Dropping the blanket, I gently peel the boot off her left foot— how the fuck she can walk in these I will never know, but fuck they make her legs look they go on for days. I reach for her right one and gently pull it off. I drop her boot to the floor when I see a tattoo on the side of her ankle.

My eyes widen to the size of dinner plates as I skim my thumb over the letter. Right there on the side of her ankle is a small *D*. I may be being presumptuous here but I'm 99.9% sure that D stands for Darius. When a shadow fills the doorway, I gently drop her foot and throw the blanket over her before turning around to see Beck standing there. I sigh, not in the mood for another one of his fucking bullshit heart to hearts. I make my way toward him and he steps back as I close the door quietly behind me. I take two steps toward my room before I stop and turn to face him. He stands there with a look on his face I can't decipher.

"Just spit it the fuck out," I snap, too tired and over everyone butting into my shit.

"She made a mistake, D. When are you going to let it go?"

"Stay out of this, Beckett. You and I both know why this shit will never happen," I say angrily.

He shakes his head in a way that makes me think the fucker is mocking me. "Maybe it's time you choose a different Williams sibling. A girl like that doesn't come around often, Darius."

"And how the fuck would you know?" He closes the space between us until we are chest to chest.

"Because I lost the best thing in my life. I was too stupid to realize how good I had it until I fucking lost it. Don't be stupid like me, because you'll spend the rest of your life regretting every choice you ever make because *she* won't be by your side. No amount of success or wealth will ever fill the void she will leave in your life."

I can't sleep!

I've been laying here for hours mulling over Beck's words. What the fuck happened in his past and who is this girl he speaks of? When I hear the adjoining bathroom door slide open, I close my eyes and feign sleep. I hear her shuffling around my room. I open my eyes to slits as I watch her head for my dresser, open the draw and pull out a shirt before quietly closing it. She turns to leave but then pauses. She slowly swivels back toward me. I keep my breathing even and lay still as she tip toes quietly over to me. I keep my eyes closed fully waiting to see what she does next, when I feel her lips press against mine it takes everything inside me not to move and remain still.

She pulls back and runs the pads of her fingers against my stubble. "I'm so sorry for everything I ever did to you," she whispers brokenly before retreating back into the bathroom and closing the door. When I hear the shower start running, I bolt upright in bed. The thought of her naked and dripping wet mere feet away from me has my restraint taut and ready to snap. If I go in there, I have to let go of the anger I harbor toward her for what she did to me. I'll also be risking my friendship with Corvin. He's warned me to steer clear of her —if I fuck it up he won't give me another chance.

Maybe it's time to choose a different Williams sibling.

Beckett's words play on a loop in my head, taunting me, daring me to take what I want. I'm still mad at her but my need to bury my cock inside her outweighs some of my anger. I throw the covers off and swing my legs over the side of the bed. I scrub my hands down my face as a war of emotions spur to life inside me.

"Fuck it!" I growl as I storm toward the bathroom. I grip the handle ready to slide it open but the sound of a moan has me pausing. I lean my ear against the door and strain my hearing. Another moan slips from her mouth.

"Oh God." A thought hits me, what if she's in there with Beckett? "Darius." The sound of my name slipping from her sinful lips has the worry fleeing my body. I edge the door open just enough for me to see her with her fingers buried inside her pussy. Her other hand is pinching her nipple. She throws her head back as another moan crawls its way out of her. My cock twitches in my boxers from seeing the water dripping down her delectable body and seeing her cheeks heat as she chases her high. Her eyes are closed as she continues to pump her fingers in and out of herself. An irrational sense of jealousy overcomes me. I'm the only one who gets to make her come. I quietly slide the door open, she's too lost in the pleasure she is inflicting on herself to notice me.

I push my boxers down my legs. My cock springs free and smacks against my stomach as I kick them to the side. I slowly creep forward and open the shower door. Her eyes snap open. Before she can scream in fright I dart into the stall and cover her mouth with my hand as I push her flush against the wall. Her eyes are wide and filled with shock and lust. The showerhead soaks me and has water dripping down my face, forcing my hair to flop against my forehead. She gingerly reaches up and pushes it back, making an involuntary shiver work its way down my spine at the feeling of her touching me.

"This is just me needing to fuck you, nothing more." Her brows bunch into the center of her face. "Can you handle that?" I slowly remove my hand from her mouth and use it to grip her waist. A small gasp slips from her lips. I know I sound like a prick but right now I can't promise her more than this. I'm not ready to jump into trying to work things out with this anger still inside me.

"I'll take you anyway I can," she says with determination. Rather than using words I answer her by slamming my mouth against hers. She opens for me like always, and the moment I push my tongue inside her mouth, a groan tears from me at the taste of her. She reaches out and runs her hands down my chest. The second her fingers skim across my cock, I break the kiss and groan as I lean my forehead against hers.

"Get on your knees and suck it." My voice is raspy and thick with need. She doesn't hesitate to do as she is told. She lowers to her knees and grips the base of my cock. She pumps it a couple times forcing me to reach out and lean my hands against the wall to keep my balance. She darts her tongue and swipes it across the head of my dick. "Fuck," I snarl as a shiver works its way up my spine. The second she wraps her lips around my cock, a strangled moan tears out of me—the girl is a pro at sucking dick. The way she swirls her tongue around the underside of my cock has my hips thrusting forward of their own accord. Unable to take her teasing, I drop one of my hands into her hair, fisting it as I begin to fuck her face without mercy. I force her to take everything I have to give. She doesn't protest, instead she grips my ass and pulls me forward until my dick is rammed all the way down her throat.

My breathing picks up, my thrusts grow unsteady. When I feel my balls begin to tighten, I rip my cock free of her mouth, grip my shaft and pump it four times, then roar out my release as I watch jets of my cum spurt all over her face and tits. I stare down at her, expecting her to be pissed at what I just did. When she swipes a finger across her cheek, wiping my cum onto the digit, she brings it to her mouth, flicks her eyes to mine and sucks it clean as she moans at the taste.

"Jesus!" I growl as I push off the wall and offer her my hand. She takes it, then steps under the spray of water with her back to me.

"You don't have to stick around," she says before ducking her head under the water. Her dismissal of me pisses me off. If she thinks her sucking my cock was enough, she is so fucking mistaken.

CHAPTER THIRTEEN

His hand grips my hair and yanks my head back drawing a strangled groan of pain from me. He pulls me toward him and gets right in my face. Water drips down his own, making him look like a literal wet dream.

"I'm not done with you," he grits out before his mouth crashes against mine. I kiss him back, pouring everything I feel for him into this kiss. His hold on my hair releases as I wrap my arms around his neck. Then his hands slide down my body to grip the back of my thighs, and hoist me up. My legs lock around his waist instinctively. He turns us so my back is against the tiled wall. The look in his eyes steals the breath from my lungs. I can see the hurt lurking beneath the surface, but the one emotion that pushes to the surface of his eyes is desire. We remain still, staring at each other for a long time. It causes a lump to form in my throat. Before I can call him on it, he plasters his mouth to mine, this time his kiss isn't hurried or angry, it's soft, slow and sensual.

I run my fingers through his hair before allowing my hands to roam his body. I touch everywhere I can. I feel him doing the same but I also know that he is doing it for the same reasons as I am—we're cementing the feeling of each other into our memory because this isn't just him and me wanting to fuck. This is his way of saying goodbye to me and this is my way of trying to convince myself that I just need to feel him one more time inside me so I can let him go. He breaks our kiss and shifts me until I feel the head of his cock at my entrance. I hold his gaze as he slowly lowers me onto him. My mouth opens as a heady moan escapes me at the feeling of having him inside me again.

Once he is buried inside me, we both sigh in contentment. He keeps his eyes on me as he slowly rocks in and out, drawing a strangled whimper from me. The longer I look into his eyes and feel his body pressed against me, it gives me everything but at the same time takes it all away. I bury my face in the crook of his neck, unable to look at him anymore—it hurts too much. Tears cascade down my cheeks. I don't understand how I can feel so heartbroken but in turn feel so fucking alive because of how amazing he is making me feel. When he thrusts inside me with more force then a second ago, I cry out. He does it again. I try to remain quiet but I can't.

"Bite me or you're going to wake your fucking brother." I do as he says and clamp down on the soft skin between his neck and shoulder. He growls at the feeling. His grip on my ass tightens as he continues to thrust inside me at the right speed. I can feel the walls of my pussy clamping down on his cock and he groans his approval. "Fuck you feel so good, Goldie," he grits out. I drag my nails down his back, drawing shudders from him. I tear my mouth off his neck and smash my lips against his, kissing him with everything I have. I feel my orgasm cresting and try to break the kiss but he won't let me. He reaches up with one of his hands, grips the back of my neck and holds me in place as he continues to pound inside me. I scream into his mouth as an orgasm so intense and raw rips through me.

He doesn't slow his pace even as I turn to jelly in his hold, his thrusts turning frantic which tells me he's close. He breaks our kiss and bites down on the tender flesh between my neck and shoulder, the same place I bit him. I cry out at the exquisite feeling that spurs to life inside me. His jaw clamps down harder as he grunts out his release. He unclenches his jaw from my shoulder sending a shiver down my spine when he places a tender kiss to the mark before resting his forehead against it. I wrap my arm around his neck and use my other hand to run my fingers through his hair. I soak in this moment and try to store the memory of what touching him feels like in my mind.

"Our hearts are wild creatures, Darius, that's why our ribs are cages." He slowly leans back so he can look at me. I wall off my emotions from him so he can't see the anguish in my eyes.

"I don't even know what that means."

"It means you can't help who you love." His brows draw in, I cup his face between my hands as I place a soft kiss to his lips then rest my forehead against his, closing my eyes. "I fucked up. I know you hate me… I hate myself for what I did to you." Tears continue to fall down my cheeks. "I'll always love you." He tenses at the sound of my whispered words. He says nothing as he slowly pulls out of me and lowers me to my feet, holding my waist until I'm steady on them. Once he's sure I'm able to stand, he withdraws his hands. I close my eyes when I feel a rush of cold air hit me, knowing he's just left. I cover my mouth with my hand and slowly drop to the shower floor hugging my knees to my chest as I cry. I have no one to blame but myself—I destroyed us.

◆

"Get up, breakfast time!" I bolt upright in bed and scream in fright. "Fuck!" I dart my gaze to the door to see Crue standing there with wide eyes. My breaths come in ragged pants as I try to calm my racing heart. The bathroom door flies open to reveal an angry looking Darius who stands there in nothing but a towel with a shirt clenched in his first. He glares at Crue then swings his gaze to me. Seeing the hickey I left on him last night on display fills me with a sense of smug satisfaction.

"Shit!" he grits out before tossing the shirt in his hand at me. I catch it before it can smack me in the face. I frown. "Cover the fuck up!" he growls. "You, get the fuck out now!" he snaps at Crue as I drop my gaze and squeal. I was hot as fuck when I crawled into bed so I'm only in a pair of panties. I race to tug the shirt over my head before I bury my face in my hands in embarrassment. "If you plan to fuck my friends, at least don't do it in my fucking house!" I snap my gaze to his, my mouth is ajar in shock that he would even think that! He shoots me a disgusted look before turning around and marching back into the bathroom, slamming the door behind himself. I stare at the closed door for so long my neck begins to cramp. I shake it off and tell myself to suck it up. I need to get used to how Darius is going to be. I did this and now I need to live with the consequences.

I sluggishly make my way downstairs, wearing my shorts and Darius's shirt while carrying my boots and top from last night in my hand. I hear conversation coming from the kitchen, so I drop my stuff on the couch before following the sounds of laughter. Crue and Saint sit at the table laughing with Beck. I dart my gaze to the other side and frown when I see Katie and Cody standing there helping Corvin plate up.

"Uh, what are you two doing here?" I ask. My friends snap their gazes to me. Katie's eyes widen and Cody pales at the sight of me. When I hear the guys laughter die off, I look at them and suddenly Crue and Saint both find their plates more interesting and can't stop looking at them. My eyes widen as I snap my gaze back to my girls, realization dawning on me. Cody steps toward me but I hold up my hand, her face falls. I open my mouth to speak when I suddenly feel Darius at my back, Corvin's face morphs into a picture of rage.

"Don't be salty, Sis. You fucked my best friend, so only fair I fucked yours." My eyes pop wide as Cody's face falls. Seeing the hurt in her eyes sends my anger soaring. I meet Corvin's angry stare with one of my own.

"You can be pissed at me all you want but you do not get to hurt Cody to get at me." I'm so proud of myself when my voice doesn't waiver.

"Nice shirt," Corvin grits out as he shoulders past me. I sigh, knowing that he won't believe me even if I told him the truth. I close the couple feet of space between me and Cody and wrap her in a hug. She tenses for a second before relaxing and returning my embrace.

"There are so many better looking guys in the world then that idiot I share DNA with," I say sarcastically. We both break out into a fit of laughter that eases the tension.

"Still better looking than you," Corvin mumbles from his seat at the table.

"That's debatable, Brother. I'd rather stare at her ass than yours." I roll my eyes, Saint is such a dork. Darius mutters something behind me before making his way into the kitchen. He reaches into the pantry to grab his protein powder and freezes, he looks to me and I cringe.

"Did you drug all of it?" I bite my lip and shake my head, suddenly feeling so unwelcome I decide it would be better if I left given Darius's remark has tension filling the room and all eyes on me.

"Thanks for the ride, Beck. I'll catch you guys later," I say as I turn and head into the living room to grab my stuff.

"Leah, wait." I don't listen, grabbing my top and shoes and head for the door. I grip the handle and pull it a quarter of the way open before Corvin reaches above my head and slams it shut. I spin around and glare at him.

"Wait for what, Corv? You want to call me a whore again? Or what is it this time, you gonna call me a junkie now since I doped your buddies?" I'm beginning to get hysterical now and I'm unable to stop myself. "You won, Corvin! I'm the fucking town bike according to the rumors. Your bestie kicked my ass to the curb, so don't worry, I'll only let the basketball team run a fucking train on me this time!" We stand here glaring at each other, not even flinching, when the sound of glass shattering can be heard from the kitchen. I blow out a tired breath and shake my head, tired of the tension and fighting. I decide to add on, "I'm going to take the rest of the semester off and take my classes online." Katie and Cody rush around the corner looking at me with horrified looks on their faces.

"Where are you going to go?" he asks. My shoulders slump. He didn't even try to convince me to stay, he wants me gone just as much as Darius, and that fucking stings.

I shrug my shoulders. "Does it matter?"

"You're my sister," he says solemnly.

"I'm not your problem, Corvin. You got your business, school, football and your friends to worry about. At least with me gone, that will be one less worry for you." When I feel tears begin to build in the backs of my eyes, I know I need to get out of here. I reach up on my tip toes and place a kiss to his cheek. "For what it's worth, Corvin, I am really sorry. I never meant to hurt any of you and I swear, I never meant to cause a rift between you and Darius," I whisper before turning and opening the door. This time, he doesn't stop me.

CHAPTER FOURTEEN

Darius

Three weeks…

"Throw the fucking ball then, you pussy!" I yell. Corvin takes his helmet off and throws it to the ground, then storms toward me. I do the same until we both smack into each other.

"You think you can do better?" he grits out through clenched teeth.

I press my forehead against his. "Yeah, I fucking do!" Corvin and I have been fighting daily over the stupidest things. None of us thought Leah was serious when she said she was leaving three weeks ago. When Corv went over to speak with her the next day, Cody slammed the door in his face after telling him it was his and *my* fault that her best friend left. She hasn't returned his calls or texts. He had no choice but to tell his mom and dad, they are worried sick. He didn't tell them why she ran just that some shit went down and she bolted. He made it seem like she just gave up, when that wasn't the fucking case at all.

"Both of you, get the hell off my field and hit the showers. You are done for the day!" Coach shouts. I shove him back and stalk off the field, heading for the locker rooms. The second I barge through the door, I throw my helmet across the room then punch the locker beside me. I grit my teeth when pain radiates up my arm.

"Hope you're pleased with yourself." I spin around and glare at Corvin. I clench my fists at my sides as he walks toward me, leaving an inch of space between us.

"Fuck you," I snarl.

"Nah, you've fucked enough Williams, I think," he snaps. I punch him right in the jaw. He stumbles back a step before he roars and charges at me, tackling me into the lockers. I grunt then drop an elbow to his back. It doesn't have the desired effect because he's still wearing his pads. He lands a solid punch to my side before I manage to shove him back. I land another hit to his face. His head snaps to the side and he spits blood on the floor. When he slowly turns back to face me, his eyes are filled with hatred as he looks at me. "You and me, we're done." He spits blood at my feet. My anger begins to dissipate, then I curse and stab a hand through my hair.

"Corvin–"

"No, Darius. You've done enough!"

"I didn't do shit!" He charges at me again, this time I don't defend myself when he hooks me in the cheek. I stumble and quickly right myself as I wait for him to come at me again.

"She was doing good… you fucking ruined it!"

"How the fuck did I ruin it?" I shout. He reaches up and tugs on the strands of his hair in frustration.

"You should have left her alone." All the anger flees my body, I decide I need to be open with him.

"I couldn't, Corvin." His gaze bores into me. I push on knowing that I need to tell him so he knows she wasn't just some random girl I was fucking. "I tried to stay away from her, I swear I did. But then after time, I couldn't bear the thought of being away from her."

"Were you fucking my sister the whole time?" I shake my head.

"No. I swear, the first time was on her sixteenth birthday." He scrubs a hand down his face.

"What the fuck happened, Darius?" I blow out a loud exhale as I dive into the story.

"I told her that we could never be more than friends because she is your little sister and was fourteen at the time, she didn't take that well." He snorts knowing how stubborn his sister is. "Then a year went by and we hung out a lot more, she started becoming… more. Then about three months before her sixteenth birthday shit changed and I couldn't deny how I felt for her. Look, shit got real and I had planned to tell you until I got to that party and saw her in bed with Gary. We fought earlier that night and in my head, I thought she assumed I had chickened out and decided to fuck me over by sleeping with him. I had no fucking idea that he had drugged her. If I had, I would have killed the bastard for hurting my girl." He quirks a brow at me.

"*Your* girl?" I don't cower, I hold his gaze as I nod my head stiffly. "How exactly did—do you feel about my sister and don't fucking lie to me?" I mull over his words for a second and decide I need to stop lying to myself.

"I've been in love with Leah since I was seventeen." His face slackens in shock at my honesty. "I thought us going away to college would help me get over her, but it didn't. I could only fuck another chick doggy because I couldn't stand the sight of their face. Shit, Corvin, the only girl I have ever kissed is Leah. I've never kissed another girl." He throws his head back and groans.

"What the fuck happened that night after you and Beck brought them back from the club." I scrunch my face. "Fucking hell, skip the dirty details." I nod.

"I… let her go," I say quietly.

"What the fuck does that mean?"

I throw my hands in the air and scowl at him. "You didn't give me a choice. You told me to stay the fuck away from her," I shout.

"Seems like you didn't listen though, huh?"

"I can't, Corvin. I fucking hate drugs and you know that, but she is a fucking addiction that I can't get rid of. She's under my skin, she's inside me," I say as I pound my fist against my chest.

"Do you still… love her?"

A whoosh of air escapes me. "Yeah, Corv, I still love her and I'm sorry I lied to you. But I have to be honest with myself, if you ask me to choose between you or her…" I hold his gaze so he can see how serious I am. "I choose her, I fucking love her and I know you will hate me for that but it's the truth. I'm done lying to myself and everyone else." He stands there silently staring at me for a long time. I begin to prepare myself for him to tell me to get out and stay away from him. It's gonna suck losing my best friend but she is worth the sacrifice.

"Help me find my sister?" My brows rise to my hairline. "Seriously?"

He narrows his eyes. "Don't fucking push me. Help me find her and then… we'll deal with this shit but, Darius?"

I swallow audibly. "Yeah?"

"You need to let go of the drug shit. You and I both fucked up. She needed us after that shit with Gary and neither of us were there for her." I hang my head in shame.

"You both might not have been, but I was." I spin around to see Beck leaning against the wall with a smug look on his face.

"How long have you been there?" Corvin demands.

Beck shrugs. "Long enough to know you two have kissed and made up." Both Corv and I snicker while Beck shrugs. Saint and Crue appear, drawing a groan from me. Clearly the three of them have been standing there listening the entire fucking time!

"So, is this the part where we tell you that Leah has been talking to Beck every day?" I snap my gaze to Beck's the second I register what Saint just said. He stands there staring directly at me, daring me to come at him. I refrain from giving into my instincts of wanting to rearrange his face.

"Where is she?" Corvin demands as he slides up beside me. Beck pushes off the wall and stands a couple feet away from us with his arms crossed over his chest. Saint and Crue stand either side of Beck mimicking his stance.

I roll my eyes over their display of power they think they have. "Spit it the fuck out or I'll beat it out of you." Beck cuts his gaze to me and narrows his eyes.

"What guarantee do I have that you two won't fuck it up again?" I grind my teeth and try to take some deep breaths through my nose to calm my temper.

"I need to apologize for being a right prick and make it up to her, please, Beck." I can tell that was hard for Corvin to say from how tense he is. Beck nods and then flicks his gaze back to me expectantly, I narrow my eyes.

"Her ass needs to get back here so I can remind her who the fuck said ass belongs to. Happy now?" No sooner have I finished speaking, than I am shoved into the lockers. I shoot Corvin a glare.

"Don't ever fucking talk about my sister's ass!" I last a whole two seconds before I laugh. Before long, the five of us are all laughing. It's been a long time since the five of us have been in a room and actually laughing, it's been nothing but tension and dirty looks for weeks.

"Okay." I turn back to Beck and wait. "I suggest you two plan something good for Thanksgiving and be ready to grovel!"

"Fucking tell me where she is!" I snap at Beckett.

He shakes his head and smirks smugly. "I was sworn to

secrecy, my dudes, plus it serves you both right to suffer for being fucking assholes." I gape at the motherfucker as he turns and walks out with the cocky duo following after him.

"I'm gonna beat their asses," Corvin growls.

"Fuck, yes!"

"Prank war?" I slowly turn to face my best friend and grin like a kid on Christmas.

"Fuck yes, those bastards are going down!"

***

Corvin and I wait out back for the three assholes to get back from practice. Excitement thrums through me when they realize what we have done! I stuff my hands into the pocket of my hoodie, the weather is starting to get colder and I couldn't be happier. I fucking love winter.

"You know Saint and Crue are going to take this to the extreme, right?" I lull my head to the side to smirk at Corvin, who is reclined on the lounger beside me.

"They can try." The sound of the front door opening alerts us to their arrival. Corvin wiggles his brows at me as we wait.

"Fuck!" We hear Crue shout, then we are both launching out of seats and racing over to peer through the back door as we watch the three of them slip all over the wooden floor. We poured oil from the front door to the stairs. Corvin and I both burst out laughing at the sight of them skating all over the place. I completely lose it when Beck begins to do the running man and falls flat on his ass.

"I'm gonna fucking kill them!" he roars from his spot on the ground. I open the back door and step inside with Corv right behind me, the three of them swinging their angry glares our way.

"Oh my goodness gracious, what is going on here?" Corvin mocks.

Saint points at the pair of us. "You're going down for this

motherfuckers." If they think this is bad, I can't wait for them to see what awaits them in their rooms.

Corvin and I decide to help them out and give them a hand. The fuckers think we are trying to suck up so they won't turn this shit around on us. Truth is, we just want them to go upstairs, which they are doing now leaving us to clean the floor. The moment the three of them turn their backs and head upstairs, Corvin and I shake with silent laughter. Once they reach the landing we move to the base of the stairs, I count to three and then it happens.

"Darius!"

"Corvin!"

"You motherfuckers!"

They all shout in unison. Corvin and I race out the back door laughing our asses off as we race around the side of the house. I push the side gate open and we make a break for Corv's car. We can still hear the three of them shouting inside. I'm laughing so hard, I have tears and my stomach is hurting. I yank the passenger door open and slip inside the car. Corvin is a second behind me, just as he slams the car into reverse I spot Beck running around the side of the house looking furious.

"Go, go, go!" I yell as he plants his foot and peels out of the driveway, with a pissed off Beckett chasing after us until we hit the end of our street.

CHAPTER FIFTEEN

Leah

Two weeks later…

"Thanks, Val, I'm so glad Katie told me about you."

"Leah, it's my pleasure, honestly. Thanks for working with my crazy schedule." I smile at Val. The girl is not only stunning with her red hair, blue eyes, and cheekbones to die for, but she is also crazy freaking smart. Since transferring to online classes my grades have slipped and I'm so behind in English. Val is my tutor. She makes everything so easy and the way she explains it to me I actually understand what it means.

"Of course. Honestly, your son is so cute so I get how you would get distracted," I say. Her son is so freaking cute. He's four, and oh my God, you can tell the boy is going to be a heartbreaker. He has tanned skin, thick black ringlets and her blue eyes—the boy is going to have a line of girls wanting his attention.

"Thanks, You, Cody and Katie seem to be the only ones who are cool with me being a mom and student." I frown.

"Seriously?" She rolls her lips over her teeth and nods.

"Yeah. I don't have friends because I can't go partying

every weekend and hit the beach whenever I want." That makes me so sad. I've never met Val in person, we talk every day over video while she tutors me. The school pays her for her time which is freaking amazing.

"Well, you have me, Cody and Katie and we don't care you can't party. You and that gorgeous boy are welcome to hang out with us anytime." Her eyes begin to fill with moisture and my heart breaks for her. Being a mom must be freaking hard, but being a mom with no support must be hell. She mentioned that Dawson's father isn't around and I never pushed for more information. I could see that was a touchy subject for her.

"Thanks, Leah, I better go bathe him and get him ready for bed." We say our goodbyes and agree to video at the same time. I really like Val. She never pushes or tries to pry into the reason why I decided to take my classes online for the rest of the semester. She seems like a genuinely nice person. Katie and Cody both adore her. I speak to my besties every day and even Nathan. He is fast becoming one of us and that makes me so happy because he truly is an amazing guy.

I close my laptop and place it on the bedside table before climbing off my bed and stretching. My shoulders are burning from spending hours sitting there working away on my papers. I peer out the window and marvel at the beautiful view, Alaska is fucking breathtaking. Five weeks ago when I walked out of my brother's house, I had no idea where I was going to go. I just knew I needed to get away and clear my head. Truthfully, I needed space away from Darius. It was killing me to see him and know that I could never have him. Beck came to my dorm that afternoon and told me to pack a bag and meet him at his car. I didn't argue. What I didn't expect was for him to hand me a plane ticket and tell me that I was going to be traveling to their resort in Alaska.

Spending the past five weeks here at this amazingly lavish resort has helped me heal so much. I found a strength within myself I didn't even know existed, which is the only reason I agreed to Beck's request of returning home for Thanksgiving. I even found the courage to call my parents last week and tell them *everything*. Mom cried, Dad lost the plot and vowed to find a way to ruin the Hayes. It took me a while to convince him that Corvin and the others have everything sorted. I told them that I was taking a break from dance and finally chose a major. My dad was happy that I decided to major in business, but mom is worried about me giving up dance. I love to dance, but after seeing what my brother and the others accomplished, it inspired me. I still want to dance but just not full time. I can't find the passion for it anymore and the reason for that is because the last time I danced it was for *him*.

My phone pings with a message. I turn away from the window and grab it off the bed, smiling when I see who it's from.

BECKY

you set for your flight tomorrow?

I think so…

BECKY

what's with the dots, babe?

Beckett has been my constant. He has been there for me daily and never judges me. I never in a million years thought I would ever become close with Beck, but here I am. I am forever indebted to him for what he has done for me. My phone rings with an incoming FaceTime from Beck and I answer without hesitation.

"Hey," I say the moment his face fills my screen. Beckett is gorgeous, there is no doubt about that. I've wondered for weeks why he couldn't be the one I had fallen for.

"Hey, beautiful, what's up?" I sigh.

"I'm nervous." His eyes fill with understanding.

"Don't be, no one knows that you are coming back." I

nibble on my bottom lip, debating if I should ask the question that has been burning in the back of my mind all day. "He doesn't know, Leah." I swear Beck is a mind reader, my shoulders slouch and I nod. "I haven't told anyone. If you don't want to see them, then you don't have to but we are doing a bonfire at the beach." This will be the first year I won't be at home for Thanksgiving. Corvin has sent our parents away on a cruise—needless to say our parents jumped at the chance. Dad has sold his business and they are finally retiring and planning to travel like they have always wanted. They wouldn't be able to do that if it wasn't for Corvin.

"Can I get back to you on that one?" I ask nervously.

"Babe, you do what is right for you. He's an idiot for letting you go. You're a diamond and if he can't see past his own pigheadedness, then he doesn't deserve you." Beckett always knows what to say to make me feel better.

"Thanks, Beck. I couldn't have done any of this without you." He smiles sadly.

"Yeah, you could have. You're strong as fuck, Leah, and what you have been through, not a lot of women would have survived it like you have." Feeling choked up, I decide to change the subject.

"How's the prank war?" Beck told me a couple weeks ago about Darius and Corvin finally making up. That same day they poured oil on the floor and then put a dozen chickens in each of the guys' rooms. Beck was furious. He said it took a week to get the smell of shit out of his room and ever since, they have been pulling pranks. It warms my heart to know that Corvin managed to work things out with Darius. I'm glad they are still best friends.

"Saint took it too far when he stole the handle bars off Darius's bike and took the spark plugs from Corvin's car, making them both late to practice. Coach made them run laps the whole time. Saint wound up with a black eye from Darius that day, so now we are at a stalemate and I fucking hope it lasts." I laugh, these boys will never fully grow up. We chat for another twenty minutes. I fill him in about my studies and tell him about the resort. He seems so excited to move here after Christmas, I am going to miss him so fucking much while he is here for six months.

Excitement thrums through me as I wheel my suitcase behind me and head toward the exit. The moment I break through the sliding doors, I spot Beckett leaning against his car. I stop in my tracks as I take in the sight of him. He wears his Ray Ban sunglasses that shield his eyes, his hair a tousled mess but in the most perfect way. He wears a dark green shirt under his leather jacket, his dark wash jeans hug his legs perfectly. I shake myself out of my staring and run toward him. He spots me when I'm a few feet away and a broad smile stretches across his face as he pushes off the car. I drop the handle of my case and launch myself into his waiting arms. I wrap my arms and legs around him as he buries his face in the crook of my neck. To people looking at us we would look like a couple but this is just... us.

"I fucking missed you, babe." His words have me melting. I lean back in his hold and smile down at him.

"I missed you too, Becky." He glares playfully at the use of my nickname for him. He swats my ass causing me to yelp in his hold. He grins up at me, causing me to roll my eyes.

"Put me down, caveman, my girls await my arrival," I say in a horrid accent that has us both laughing. Beck and I spend the drive back to CHU catching up and laughing. It's so easy with him. I would have thought us having sex would have complicated things but it didn't. If anything, it has brought us closer. I admit, Beck is fucking hot, but I don't have that burning sensation in my belly when I'm near him. His touch doesn't set me ablaze or have me squirming. We pull into the carpark of CHU, nerves thrum through me. Beck parks the car and doesn't move to get out, instead he reaches across and clasps my hand in his giving a squeeze.

"They aren't here," he says softly.

"Do they…" I exhale loudly and pluck up the courage to ask him what I really want to know. "Does *he* know I'm back?" Beck reaches over with his free hand and clasps my chin in his hand as he slowly turns my face toward him.

"I told them to plan something good for Thanksgiving and that was it. They have no idea you're here." I nod as I nibble my bottom lip. Beck pries it free with his thumb before brushing the pad of his thumb along my lip.

"Why couldn't it be you." My eyes widen when I realize I said that out loud, and his eyes soften.

"You and me fit too well to work, babe." I frown, not understanding what he's saying. "You need someone who is going to fight you and not cave to your demands when you bat your lashes and shake your ass. I would cave in a second." I giggle which draws a sad smile to his face. "Darius won't. He will fight you and tie your ass down and say fuck it to the repercussions."

"He hates me, Beck," I whisper brokenly.

"He was hurt. He has trust issues because of how he was brought up. Give him a chance to explain it to you and I promise you, it will make things clear. He is going through a lot right now. Gary is trying to sue him." I gasp.

"What the fuck, why?"

"He says that Darius has cost him his future and is suing him for money lost or some shit. Troy's on it now but it's just a lot."

"I bet."

"Look, you have girls waiting for you, so get your cute ass out of my car and enjoy your night with the girls. If you change your mind, we're doing a bonfire and picnic at the beach tomorrow for Thanksgiving. Classes are out for the holidays so there won't be a lot of people there." I nod.

"I'll think about it."

"Perfect, but there is a dress code."

I frown. "What do you mean?"

"Saint made it a dress up party and it's swimwear or lingerie." I roll my eyes, of course Saint would make it a dress up party so he could spend the night checking out every piece of ass.

CHAPTER SIXTEEN

Darius

The five of us walk out of our last practice until after the break. I love football but fuck me, I'm glad to be having a break. In two weeks' time we have our next game and I am chomping at the bit to be back on the field under the spotlights running the length of the field.

"Hey, stranger." I grind to a stop when Chelsea darts in front of me, her sickly scent of perfume assaults my nose. I fight the gag that wants to break free.

"Oh look, it's a stray," Crue sing songs beside me. Chelsea cuts him a glare as some of her friends come to stand with her, all standing tall and popping their chests out, trying to garner our attention.

"Hey, Darius." I frown at the brunette behind Chelsea. I have no idea who the girl is but her greeting brings a dark look to the nasally bitch's eyes in front of me.

"Sup," I reply just to fuck with her.

"So, we heard about the party tomorrow and can't wait." I cut Saint a dark look, he shrugs.

"Dude, it was an open invite to whoever is staying behind." I shake my head.

"Cool, see ya then," I grit out as I try to step around her

but she blocks my path. A growl of annoyance tears from me as I pin her with a warning look.

"I know Leah being back must upset you, so I can stop by later if you'd like me to make you feel better?" She is misreading the look on my face, she reaches out and rests her hand on my chest in fake support. "She is such a bitch!" she hisses. Corvin saddles up next to me and pushes her hand off me.

"That bitch is my sister, you fucking cunt." Chelsea gasps at Corvin's harsh words. I don't stick around, I use her shock to my advantage and take my leave with the others following after me. My mind is reeling. Leah's back. I head for the carpark, jump on my bike and don't wait for the others as I peel out of the lot heading straight for her dorm building. It takes me less than five minutes before I'm pulling into the carpark of her building. I park my bike and march toward her building, but when the sound of laughter hits my ears, laughter that I know all too well, I follow the sound around the side of the building and freeze. I keep to the shadows as I watch her, Cody and Katie do cartwheels on the quad. A smile breaks free at the sight of her. I'm about to make my presence known, but stop when I hear him.

"Looking good." I pin the motherfucker with a death glare even though he can't see me. Now, I get why the fucker wasn't at practice, he blew us off to hang with my girl.

"Garrett, you are so good for my ego," Leah says as she laughs. I hate the way he looks at her. He thinks he has the right to run his eyes over her body, when he fucking doesn't.

"Well, I'm beat and going to call it a night," Katie announces.

"Same," Cody chimes in. Leah opens her mouth to speak but Garrett beats her to it.

"Have dinner with me." My blood turns to ice inside my body as I implore her with my mind to say no. She looks taken back by his offer. That's a good thing, right?

"Nope, I am not dealing with Beckett pounding down my door the second he hears she went out with you so nope, Leah stays with us!" Leah seems to relax and shoots Cody a grateful look. I'm starting to like Cody more and more now.

"Leah's a big girl, she can make up her own mind," Garrett says. My fist aches to smash his face.

"I'm beat from the long flight back from Alaska." *Alaska?* Beckett, you son of a bitch. "I'll catch up with you tomorrow?" It brings me great joy to see the crestfallen look on his face at her rejection.

"Yeah, okay," he says dejectedly. Leah gives him a quick hug before heading toward me. I turn and race back to the carpark to avoid being seen. I'll give her tonight, but come tomorrow I plan to take back what is mine!

I barge through the front door of my house heading straight for the kitchen ,knowing that's where he will be. Sure enough, there he stands laughing at something Corvin said. They all turn toward me the moment I enter. I march toward him and hit him. He stumbles back into the counter. Corvin jumps in the middle of us and shoves me back a step. I glare at Beckett over his shoulder. Saint and Crue rush over to check on Beckett who is cupping his mouth.

"What the fuck?" Corvin yells in my face. I keep my glare on Beckett as I answer him.

"That fucker sent her to Alaska!" I shout. Corvin spins around to face Beck, who drops his hand and shoots us a bloody smirk. His lip is split and that gives me great satisfaction.

"You sent my sister to *our* resort?" Corvin demands.

"Sure did and it was genius. Neither of you thought to look for her there, did you?" I try to rush him again but Corvin blocks me.

"You are going to pay for that!" I growl. Beckett pushes forward but Saint and Crue hold him back.

"Fuck you. She needed that time away. She healed there, Darius. She is happy again and darkness doesn't shine in her eyes anymore."

"She will never be yours, Beckett. She's mine!" Corvin growls but remains silent. "You think because I let you fuck her that you have any type of claim over her?" The moment his eyes widen and Saint and Crue snap their horrified stares to me, I realize I just fucked up, badly.

"You did what now?" Corvin asks in a deadly calm tone that has me backing up a step.

"Oh shit," I hear Crue mutter.

"I-we… It's not what it sounds like–" Corvin cuts off my rambling as he turns so he can keep Beck and I both in his sights.

He points to both of us as he says, "You *both* had a fucking threesome with *my* sister?" I flinch, Beckett drops his chin to his chest. "Answer me!" Corv yells.

"Yes," I answer, while Beck nods his head.

"Jesus Christ!" Corvin snaps as he scrubs a hand down his face. We all stand here silently as Corv processes what he just learned. He looks to Saint and Crue and pins them with a harsh look that has them both raising their hands in surrender and taking a step away from Beck.

"Nope. Never touched her," Crue rushes to say.

"I talk shit about doing her but swear to God, never laid a hand on her," Saint rushes to add.

"Oh, that's great so only two out of four of my best friends have fucked my sister." I fight the cringe that wants to break free.

"It isn't how it sounds, Corvin. I would never hurt Leah," Beck says as he stares at Corvin.

"How am I supposed to believe that?" Beck flicks his gaze to me briefly before answering Corvin.

"Who has she been talking to everyday? I'm the one she has been coming to for help, not any of you."

"You both are so fucked," Corvin breaths out as he storms out of the room, making sure to shoulder check me on his way out.

"Fuck!" I rasp out. I just fucked up again. Beck presses up to me, I hold his stare waiting for him to bust a move.

"Stop trying to find someone to blame for how shit turned out. You want to be pissed, be pissed at yourself because this is on you." His words hit me hard.

"Did you mean it?" I ask cautiously.

"Mean what?" he asks, slightly confused.

"That she's happy?" He sighs and places a hand on my shoulder.

"If you're asking me if she is over you, then just ask." I suck up my pride and hold his stare.

"Has she moved on?" I can hear the sadness in my own voice, my heart is beating so fast as I wait for his reply.

He gives me a dry stare. "Dude, I know she has a tattoo on her leg with the letter D." My eyes widen in surprise that he knows about that. I mean, I assumed it was for me but I never got that confirmed. "A girl doesn't just tattoo a guy's name on her, then move on. She loves you, Darius, but she hates that she can't let you go. If you want her back, then you need to work your ass off because she won't forgive you easily."

"She straight up has his name tattooed on her?" Saint butts in but we ignore him. "Corvin is going to lose his shit!" Beckett's phone begins to ring. When he tenses, I slam my eyes closed and take a step back nodding my head.

"Answer it," I say in a defeated tone. He sucks in a sharp breath as he pulls it out of his pocket and answers.

"Hey, beautiful." I clench my fists at my sides at his endearment. Unable to listen to their conversation, I decide to call it a night and hope like hell she decides to come tomorrow night.

I feel like a pubescent teen with how fucking nervous I am. I'm even drinking to try calm the fucking nerves inside me. We've been sitting at the beach for a couple hours, some of the team is here and other students from CHU crowd around us, but I don't hear a fucking word any of them say, too focused and keeping a look out for my girl. Beck gave me a heads up this morning and told me she is going to come tonight. Ever since then, I have been a fucking wreck. Corvin hasn't killed me yet, so I'm hoping that means he isn't pissed at me for what happened with me, Leah and Beck.

"Looking good, handsome." I roll my eyes heavenward, this girl just won't fucking quit. I look at her and grit my teeth in disgust. She stands before me with a lacy lingerie set on with garters and all. I mean we're at a fucking beach. I look past her to see her skanks have all dressed the same.

"Look…" The words die in my mouth the moment I see her break through the crowd. Her long blonde hair is out and blows in the wind, her eyes bright and vibrant. Her lips are glossy and perfect. I run my gaze down her body, noting she has a black, one-piece swimsuit on with the sides cut out, leaving her hips and ribs on display. When she turns to the side to say something to Katie, I see the back of her swimsuit is open. The wind blows her skirt thing up and I have to bite my lip to keep my groan from breaking free when I see it's one of those G-string swimming suits that show off her ass cheeks. She turns around again with a smile that is so infectious I find myself smiling as well, but it drops off my face when I see Garrett step up beside her and wrap an arm around her waist.

"They actually look cute together," the annoying bitch says. I ignore her as I march toward Leah, ready to rip her off Garrett, until Corvin steps in front of me.

"Move," I growl.

"I hate him more than you but believe me, I know my sister and you will just piss her off." I cut my gaze to him. "It's going to take me a minute to adjust to the fact you're into my sister but I saw the second she arrived you shifted, your eyes told me everything, Darius."

"And what exactly did they tell?" I push.

His eyes darken. "That you really are in love with her and she isn't just some girl to you."

I feel a weight lift off my shoulders, he gets it now. "She never was just some girl to me." He sighs and nods his head.

"Then, let's make a plan to get you *your* girl back, because if you thought I was pissed finding out about you and her, you would hate to see what I would be like if I found out she was dating Garrett." I narrow my eyes.

"I'll break his fucking arm as well if he ever touches her." Corvin smiles wide and smacks me on the shoulder as he says.

"My man."

CHAPTER SEVENTEEN

We've been here not even five minutes and Garrett has his arm wrapped around me like we're a *thing*. We are so not together and I hate that he does this. I told him earlier when he showed up at the dorm with Nathan to walk us here, that I wasn't looking for more than friendship. He said he got it. Clearly, he doesn't. The second I spot Beck walking toward me with a grin on his face, I yank free of Garrett's hold and race toward Beck. I fling myself at him and he catches me around the waist with ease. He buries his face in the crook of my neck. I feel him smiling.

"You looked like you needed an out," he says as he puts me back on my feet. I shoot him a grateful smile.

"I totally did, you're a lifesaver!" I answer as the girls come up beside me. The girls greet Beck before turning to me.

"Coming for a sunset swim?" I nod eagerly, Cody knows I will never turn down a chance to swim in the ocean. I turn back to Beck.

"Want to come with?" He shakes his head and smiles.

"Nah, you girls go have fun. Come find me when you're done and I'll get you a drink." I reach on my tip toes and plant a kiss on his cheek.

"You're the best, Becky!" I shout as the three of us race off toward the water. I untie my sarong and drop it on the sand before racing after my friends. The feeling of the waves crashing into me and the smell of the sea in the air has me feeling happy. I missed this.

"Touchdown!" I hear shouted behind me before being tackled into the water. I shove the person away from me and break the surface to yell at whoever it is until I'm met with the cheesiest grin. "Baby girl, that ass was begging to be put down." I throw my head back and laugh at Nathan, he is fast becoming one of the girls. I have no idea how he and Garrett became friends considering how different they are, but thanks to Garrett, I now have another friend. I tried to get Val to come tonight but she said Dawson had a cold. She promised to come next time. The four of us stay in the water until long after the sun has set. I didn't know how much I needed this, just to be surrounded by my friend's and be a teenager without the weight of the world on my shoulders.

"Boo boo." I swing around to face Nathan, who has a mischievous look on his face.

"What's up?" I ask hesitantly.

"If you can't feel Mr. Tall Dark and Handsome's gaze on you, then there is something wrong with you, baby." I tense, I've been ignoring the feeling of having his eyes on me the whole time we have been in the water. I know if I turn around I'll find him standing there and I'm not ready, not yet. Nathan wraps his arms around me and pulls me into a hug. I wrap my arms around him and rest my cheek against his naked chest. "I got you. I also know Garrett is trying to bust a move on you."

"I don't like him like that," I say honestly.

"I know which is why I am going to tell you to be careful." I pull back and frown up at him.

"What do you mean?"

"Garrett and I have known each other for a long time.

Over the years we have drifted apart, since I got into cheer and him into football. Rumors circulate fast around here and some of the things I have heard aren't good."

"Things like?" I press. I feel Cody and Katie creep in closer to us listening.

"He gets rough with girls."

I gasp. "But you're his friend." Nathan shakes his head.

"The night I met you at the club I came with Alex, not Garrett, and the only reason I came tonight is because of you three. Garrett showed up outside your dorm on his own accord." That throws me, Garrett said earlier that he and Nathan didn't want us walking alone making it seem like they had discussed that plan earlier.

"My nipples are hard and I need a drink," Cody says, causing us all to laugh and agree. We make our way back to shore. I snag my sarong on our way back toward the partygoers. As far as Thanksgivings go, this would have to be one of the best I have had in years. Beck spots us and nods before disappearing to get us drinks, I assume. I'm proven right when he appears carrying four red cups. We all thank him as we each grab a cup and cheers before taking a sip.

"Want me to help you with your wrap?" I close my eyes and pray for patience. I slowly open them and turn to face Garrett who has pushed Nathan out of his spot beside me.

"I'm—"

"She's good, I got her," Beck says in a tone that has me standing straighter. Garrett cuts Beck a dark look before turning back to me with a warm smile on his face, but it doesn't reach his eyes. Before he can say another thing, Cody screams and shoves her cup at Garrett, forcing him to hold it or risk the contents spilling on him.

"This is our jam," she shouts as she drags me and Nathan with Katie following us to the center of the crowd where students are dancing. When I hear the words of the song, I burst out laughing. Little Mix's "Shout Out to My Ex" blares from the speakers that are set up. The four of us form a circle of sorts as we dance. I let loose and allow myself to enjoy this moment with my friends. When the next song plays, I feel giddy. Fifth Harmony's "All in My Head (Flex)" has me feeling the beat and moving my hips. Nathan whistles as he steps up behind me, grips my waist and rocks his hips in time with mine. He's plastered against my back and I feel nothing, I'm not worried he will expect something or want more, we're just two friends dancing. I mean, for goodness sake, I'm rubbing my ass against his dick and the guy is as soft as butter.

I look at my girls and I'm surprised to see a guy dancing with Katie, before I can even get a look at the guy he's shoved out of the way and replaced by Crue. Katie opens her mouth ready to have a go at him no doubt, but then he stuns the fuck out of me when he grips the back of her neck and holds her in place as he smashes his lips to hers. Cody squeals and claps for our girl while I stand here stunned. Katie wraps her arms around Crue's neck, I'm about to turn away and give them a moment but Saint plasters himself against her back, and grips her waist. I expect Crue to pull back but he doesn't. Feeling like I'm intruding on a private moment, I turn back to Cody but falter when I see my brother standing next to her with his gaze on me. We stand here still as statues just staring at each other. My feet move of their own accord and take me toward him. He meets me halfway and wraps me in a bone-crushing hug. I fight back the tears that want to fall as I bury my face in his chest clutching his shirt in my fists.

He drops a kiss to the top of my head resting his chin there. "I missed you, Lee." I inhale a shuddering breath.

"I missed you too," I choke out. I close my eyes and will my tears to not fall. I promised myself I wouldn't cry. I've cried too much these past couple months and I'm not a crier.

"I'm so sorry, Leah." I pull back but keep my grip on his shirt as he holds my arms, I can see the sincerity in his eyes. "I should have been there for you and I wasn't. I was too caught up on the whole you and Darius thing. I was a fucking poor ass excuse for a brother, can you ever forgive me?" The tenderness in which he speaks, I know he means what he says. I pull him to me and hug him tight.

"I love you, Corv, and of course I forgive you." I feel the tension in his body evaporate at my words.

"I love you too." We stand here for a minute just holding each other. "I know we just made up and shit but I have to ask…" I release him and take a step back, cringing when I see his white shirt is soaked thanks to me.

I quirk a brow at him, prompting him. "Just ask whatever it is," I say.

His eyes widen mockingly as he forces a shudder through his body. "What the fuck are you wearing and why in God's good name is your ass out?" I can't help it, I throw my head back and laugh so hard that tears leak from the corner of my eyes. I can hear Cody laughing along with me, our laughter reaches new heights when Nathan says.

"Because her ass is a peach and even gay men want to take a bite." Corvin's face pales.

"Nah, fuck that," he grumbles, grips Cody's hand and begins to lead her away. I stare at their blacks wondering what the hell is going on between them, clearly in the five weeks I have been away my friends have been *busy*.

"Well, I guess you're stuck with me," Nathan says, garnering my attention and snapping me out of my shock. I turn around and smile ready to dance some more but the moment the song switches, the smile drops from my face and my whole body begins to heat. The hairs on the back of my neck stand up alerting me to the fact he is near. The second Nathan's eyes crinkle at the corners and a sly smirk graces his face, I know he's behind me. I close my eyes and will myself to be strong—I can do this.

His hands grips my exposed waist. The feeling of his

hands on me, sets my body ablaze. He presses in until his chest is flush against my back, bends down and a shiver trails down my spine when I feel his lips brush against the shell of my ear. "Move for me, Goldie." Those four words have me obeying his command, Ella Mai's voice sounds out around us. This song is becoming ours. I sway my hips side to side, he keeps pace with me. The second I press my ass harder against him, his grip tightens and he groans in my ear. He keeps one hand on my waist and slips the other around my front to hold me closer. "You wear this for me?" he whispers huskily in my ear.

"No. I wore it for me." I'm so fucking proud of myself, my voice is strong and doesn't waiver. I expect him to shove me away and storm off like he normally does, the fact he is here dancing with me out in the open where Corvin can spot us, tells me he either doesn't care if we're caught or he's stupid.

"I want you," he says, his words have need coiling inside me. If my suit wasn't wet from my swim earlier, it would be damp with my arousal now. I want him so bad but I also can't deal with his hot and cold behavior. I turn in his hold. His eyes shine with need, need for me. He reaches around me and grips my ass covering it with his hands, I gasp. "No one gets to see this but me." My jaw slackens, his words and his nearness have my rationale short circuiting. He doesn't give me a chance to pull myself together or formulate a rational thought, his mouth is on mine in the next second. The feeling of his soft lips meshed against mine has an involuntary moan slipping from me. He uses that to his advantage and slips his tongue inside my mouth. The taste of him has me, reevaluating my plan. The second he tries to deepen the kiss a throat clearing from beside us has me pulling back and out of his hold. He shoots me a pissed off look, fuck it's so easy to give into him.

"I think you dropped this." Garrett holds out my sarong. I grab it from him and smile my thanks before quickly securing it around my waist. The tension between Darius and Garrett is so thick it's suffocating.

"There you are." I dart my gaze to the side of Darius to see Chelsea making her way toward him. She shoots me a scathing look as she stands beside him. Garrett moves to my side, I refuse to allow my judgment to slip and ruin my night. I suck in my pride, smile at Darius and shrug my shoulders. He's grinding his teeth so hard I think he may actually break them.

"See you around," I say as I turn to leave, but he snakes his arm out, grips my wrist and yanks me to him. Garrett steps forward ready to protest but Darius beats him to speak first.

"I'll break your fucking jaw before you can utter a word. Learn your place asshole, because it isn't beside her."

"Babe," Chelsea says in a sickly sweet voice. I narrow my eyes at Darius as I yank my arm free much to his dismay.

"Your girlfriend is calling you," I grit out before walking off, leaving him and that tramp alone. Anger simmers inside me at the thought of that bitch with her hands all over him. So, I do the only thing I can think of and find Beck. One look at me and he hands me the hip flask he had in the side of his board shorts. I take it, unscrew the cap and skull. It burns my throat but in the best possible way. It's stupid to drink away my issues but fuck it, YOLO.

CHAPTER EIGHTEEN

Darius

I have watched her all night. She's drunk that hip flask herself and is going to have the worst fucking hangover tomorrow. Beckett has remained by her side all night while she dances. Cody appeared about three minutes after Corvin did, with messy hair and sand caked to the back of her head, it doesn't take a genius to figure out what they were doing. Since Cody and Katie have been back she has been dancing. It pisses me off to see all the guys with their eyes on her. Everyone went nuts before when she jumped onto that guy Nathan and started grinding on him while he held her. The only reason that fucker isn't picking his teeth up off the floor is because he bats for the other team and I know he isn't interested in her.

She starts to sway on her feet. I lurch forward but Beckett is there to catch her and swing her into his arms bride style. I'm angry, frustrated and horny as fuck, those three things mixed together isn't a good cocktail. I stalk over to Beck to find Leah passed out in his arms, she looks so beautiful it hurts.

"I'm gonna take her back to her dorm." I cut my gaze to him and shake my head.

"No. She comes home with us," I say in a matter of fact tone.

"Nuh uh, she made me promise not to let any of you take her back to your house," Katie says as she steps up beside Beck, Cody and Nathan stand next to her nodding.

"And where the fuck are you staying?" I snap at Nathan, the bastard bats his lashes.

"Well, under you of course." I choke on my spit. Beckett shakes with silent laughter and the girls find humor in my horrified face as they begin to laugh. "I'm staying with them. Trust me, gorgeous, your girl does not get my cock hard." I shudder at the thought of what does get him hard.

"Right, well I'm taking her home," Beck announces. I turn to follow after him but the sound of my name being shouted has the five of us pausing, Beck turns his head toward me and says in a stern tone. "Deal with that shit now." I grit my teeth and nod. Turning around, I spy Chelsea rushing toward me. She stops a foot away and smiles suggestively at me, but before she can utter a word I decide to lay it out.

"Take the fucking hint, you and me are never going to happen. The thought of you has my cock shriveling up, you were nothing but a hole to get me off. Jesus, I couldn't even get hard to use said hole." We have garnered the attention of the bystanders but I don't care, I've tried to get her to take a hint but she won't.

"You asshole, go waste your time on that washed up slut then!" Anger soars inside me, but before I can do anything or say something, a blur of brown hair whizzes past me, then punches Chelsea right in the nose. She drops to the sand like a sack of shit, screaming as she cups her bleeding nose.

"Call my friend a slut again, you washed up twat, and next time I'll make sure I break your fucking nose!" I stare at the back of Cody's head, stunned and proud as fuck. I didn't think the girl had it in her. Everyone around us erupts into cheers at the catfight. Cody turns on her heal and marches away, grabbing me by the arm and pulling me along with her.

"Well, baby girl, I did not see that coming," Nathan says proudly as he wraps an arm around Cody's shoulders.

"Neither did I. I'm sick of all of them calling her a slut when they don't know the fucking truth. They think because she was hooking up with Darius and a video of her being raped got aired that it somehow makes her a slut." I tune them out, unable to hear anymore. As we reach the road, Leah stirs in Beck's hold, a drunken smile breaks free as she stares up at him.

"I love you, Becky." *Becky?* Beckett snorts and shakes his head.

"Love you too." It amazes me how easily they can say those words to each other.

"You're so pretty, Becky." I keep my gaze forward and watch as Nathan and the girls stumble ahead of us, out of the three of them, Cody is the least drunk.

"That's those beer goggles talking, babe," he answers.

"Why can't you be *him*," she says sadly. I see Beck tense out of the corner of my eye. "He doesn't love me." Pain erupts inside me.

"Yeah, he does, babe. I told you before, you need to talk to him." She snorts and closes her eyes.

"No, he doesn't. He just wants to fuck me, then throw me away like last time." I dart in front of Beck making him slam to a stop. I don't ask his permission as I pull her to me and carry her back to her dorm. She lazily blinks her eyes opens. When a small frown mars her beautiful face she says, "You're not my Becky." Beckett snorts beside me.

"Nah, I'm not," I say. I hold her closer against my chest and she snuggles into me.

"You're prettier than Becky." That has a laugh tearing out of me and earning myself a whack on the back of the head from *Becky*.

"Yeah, I am way hotter than him, Goldie."

"I'm horny." Beckett and I both slam to a stop, I look to the heavens praying for strength.

"She's drunk."

"I'm aware, captain fucking obvious," I say as I force my feet to move. Within a second she is fast asleep in my arms. We reach her dorm way quicker than I would have liked. I follow Katie in as Cody holds the door open for us. I glare at her futon on the floor. "When the fuck is your dorm opening again?" I ask as I lay her gently on the mattress.

"After the break," Cody says, I can hear the annoyance in her voice. I pull the cover over her and brush her hair from her face, she smiles in her sleep.

"Darius?" she mumbles, I see Katie and Cody jumping into one of the beds and Nathan hops in the other.

"Yeah?" I answer.

"I love you." My breath gets caught in my throat, I know they all heard that, I can feel their eyes on me, waiting to see what I'll do next. I lean down and place a soft kiss to her forehead.

"I love you too," I whisper.

I wake the next morning feeling lighter than I have in weeks. The sun is out and the weather isn't too cold. I decide to cook breakfast for the guys. I've been a dick lately and need to make it up to them, and the quickest way to do that is through their stomachs. An hour goes by, while I slave away in the kitchen, when the four of them finally start to trickle in.

"Oh my heart, he cooks too."

"Ha ha, asshole," I say to Saint's stupid ass comment.

"Something smells good," Beck says before he yawns, then makes his way over to the coffee pot that I just finished making.

"Pour me one!" Crue calls to Beck as he takes the seat next to Saint. Corvin is the last to walk in, his hair is a mess and he looks like a dogs ass.

"I'm never drinking again." The four of us laugh at his dumb ass statement.

"Yeah and I'll never eat another pussy," Saint mocks. Too hungover to even reply, he flips Saint off over his shoulder.

"What's the plan for the day?" Beck asks as he hands everyone a cup of coffee. I thank him before answering.

"I invited the girls and Nathan over to hang out for the day." I focus back on cooking the eggs avoiding their stares.

"Huh, which girls exactly?" I turn and pin Crue with a dry stare.

"You might know one of them, yeah I think you do actually. She was the one grinding on both your cocks last night?" Saint grins proudly, while Crue ducks his gaze to look at the table.

"Well, if I recall Katie wasn't the only girl getting some action," Saint quips. Corvin pins me with a dark look.

"Dude, Leah was fucking wasted," he admonishes. I quirk a brow and shake my head.

"My cock was in my pants all night and they weren't talking about *my* girl, they were talking about *yours*!" Corvin's eyes widen for a second before he schools his features. He can't fool me, he's trying to act like he doesn't care about Cody but I saw him last night watching her every move—he couldn't keep his eyes off her. Which leaves me to wonder, why isn't he making shit official?

"After breakfast I'll head out and get some shit. We'll have a cookout today and chill out in the pool." We all agree with Beck, that actually sounds like a great idea.

"So, will anyone be using the *spare* room tonight?" Crue taunts. I look to the heavens praying for strength not to beat his ass.

"Shut the fuck up. I don't want to hear, see or know

anything, at least that way I can pretend my sister is still a virgin." I snort and Beck coughs to masks his laughter. "I fucking hate you both," Corv moans as he moves to join the other two at the table.

"He is going to cockblock you bad," Beck says, low enough for only me to hear.

"I know and I already have blue balls," I whine.

Just before lunch time, a knock sounds at the door. Before any of the others get off their asses, I'm already halfway across the room shouting that I'll get it. I ignore their mocking laughter as I swing the door open, the smile drops off my face when I only see Cody, Katie and Nathan standing there.

"Well clearly we only got invited because of a certain blonde," Nathan taunts.

"Where's Leah?" I ask.

Cody rolls her eyes and pushes past me. "She'll be here soon," she calls over her shoulder. I look back to Katie for an explanation, she sighs and takes pity on me.

"She went to Garrett's to get her phone, I forgot to grab it off him last night for her." I nod, my good mood has slipped as I step aside and let them in. Nathan pauses in front of me, he says nothing as he waits for Katie to be out of ear shot.

The normal carefree look in his eyes is gone, a serious look overshadows his face. "You may not like me or my relationship with Leah but you need to know, I care about her and won't let a little dick like you hurt her." My brows raise to my hairline surprised he had the balls to man up to me. "Word of advice, whatever is holding you back, let it go before she lets *you* go." I stand here staring at his retreating form for a solid minute before I snap myself out of it.

An hour passes by and Leah is still nowhere to be seen, worry begins to churn inside me, I can't explain it but something doesn't feel right. I sit here on the edge of the pool while the others swim and laugh, without Leah here I have nothing to smile about. When the sound of Ella Mai's "Watchamacallit" pierces the air, I jump to my feet and rush over to the lounger. I set her ringtone to our song the night she gave me a lap dance. I hit answer and place it on speaker as I dry myself with my towel.

"Hey, Godlie."

"Darius!" I turn to stone, my blood freezes in my veins at the sound of fear in her voice. I drop the towel and pick the phone up. I feel the guys closing in around me.

"Baby, what's wrong?" I try to remain calm so I don't scare her.

"Darius, I need you!" she screams, I hear glass shatter in the background, she screams in fright.

"Leah, where are you?" I shout.

"Stop, please no—" she screams then the line goes dead. I hit redial immediately but it goes to voicemail. I try again, only to get the same thing. I throw my phone across the yard growling.

"Where the fuck is my sister?" Corvin yells, I turn to the pool where the girls lean against the edge looking horrified.

"I don't know, she said she was just going to get her phone and then come straight here," Cody says, her voice thick with worry. Nathan leaps out of the pool with a murderous look on his face, I rush over to him, wrap my hand around his throat and slam him against the banister of the deck getting right in his face.

"You have three seconds to tell me where the fuck my girl is or I'll start breaking your bones." He doesn't cower or flinch.

"I have a feeling Garrett finally snapped. I think she's with him."

"He's fucking dead!" I snarl.

CHAPTER NINETEEN

I skip up the path that will lead me to Garrett's frat house, guys sit on the porch laughing. I walk through the open door and look side to side for Garrett but can't spot him anywhere.

"You looking for Garrett?" a boy calls from the living room.

"Yeah," I answer.

"Upstairs, last door at the end of the hall," he calls out.

"Thanks," I mutter as I head up the stairs. I don't like the idea of going to his bedroom but I need my phone. The quicker I get it, the quicker I can get the hell out of here, I tell myself. My head is pounding, no amount of painkillers or water is getting rid of this bad boy and I have no one to blame but myself for being an idiot and thinking I could handle Jack. I follow the guy's directions and head toward the end of the hall. I stop outside the door, take a deep breath and square my shoulders as I reach up and knock.

"It's open," Garrett calls out. I turn the handle and open the door. Garrett sits at the desk in the corner of his room, shirtless. When he spots me in the doorway he lurches out of his seat clearly surprised to see me. "Leah."

"Hey," I say awkwardly.

"What are you doing here?"

"Uh, I forgot to get my phone off you last night." The smile on his face falters slightly.

"Yeah, of course." He sounds annoyed and I feel like an ass. He moves across his room to his dresser where my phone sits. He grabs it, instead of handing it over he holds it hostage in his hand. "Leah, can we talk?"

A resigned sigh escapes me as I nod. I like Garrett, he's a nice guy. Even while I was away he would send me his calculus notes, which was sweet of him. Except, he had no idea I switched majors and no longer take that class, thank God! He waves his arm toward the bed to have a seat, I act like I didn't see where he was pointing and sit on the chair he just vacated. His lips pinch in annoyance. I brush it off, not able to deal with his mood and my headache. He kicks the door closed before he drops on the edge of the bed with his arms resting on the tops of his thighs.

"I really don't have long, I'm meeting my brother–" I clamp my mouth closed when his upper lip pulls back and his eyes darken. Fear begins to swirl in my belly.

"Where did you sleep last night?" He tries to mask the anger in his tone but fails.

"In my own bed," I answer hesitantly. Garrett leans forward and I push back further into the chair wanting to put as much distance between us as I can.

"Huh, Chelsea said she saw you leave with Darius." I frown.

"And if I did, why would that bother you?" His eyes narrow.

"How many times does he have to treat you like shit before you realize that he is no good for you?" Fear works its way up my throat. I dart my gaze toward the closed door wondering if I would be able to make a break for it before he catches me.

"Garrett," I say softly, trying to ease his anger. "I'm not with Darius."

"But you want to be!" I recoil at the sound of his booming voice.

"I think I should leave," I say as I attempt to climb to my feet. He shoves me back into the chair. I snap my gaze to his in fright, this was a bad idea, I should have listened to my gut. Nathan's warning from last night springs to mind. I'm such a fool! Garrett leans into me, his nose brushes mine, he drops my phone into my lap as he cups my face. Before I can shove him back he smashes his lips against mine. Immediately my mind screams at me to push him back, I try but his grip on my face tightens. I feel his tongue prod at my lips trying to gain entry, and a thought hits me. I open my mouth and fight not to gag when his tongue slips inside. He moans, then I bite down on his tongue as hard as I can. He tries to yank free but I won't let go. When he slaps me across the face I release his tongue as I tumble off the chair and hit the floor. He stumbles away from me, covering his bleeding mouth. I spy my phone and grab it, I quickly unlock it and don't even hesitate to dial his number.

"Hey, Goldie."

"Darius!" I scream, Garrett darts his gaze to me and I panic.

"Baby, what's wrong?"

"Darius, I need you!" I shout as Garrett storms toward me. I shuffle back on my ass as fast as I can along the floor.

"Leah, where are you?" I hear Darius shout, Garrett cocks his arm back.

"Stop, no please—" I scream as he hits me again. My phone goes flying out of my hand, my ear ringing from the force of his hit. He stomps on my phone, smashing the screen before he turns back to me. He grips a handful of my hair and yanks me to my feet. I cry out in pain. He uses his grip on my hair to throw me across the room. I smack into his shelf before hitting the ground, the contents from his shelf lands on me, drawing a pained whimper from me.

"You like whoring around, do you?" he screams as he grips my hair and drags me along the floor. Tears cascade down my face as I try to free myself. He pulls me to my feet by my hair, I cry out when I feel strands of my hair ripped from my head. The look in his eyes is one I've never seen before, he's unhinged and clearly lost the plot.

"Garrett," I whimper. He bares his teeth at me before spitting right in my face.

"I tried to be nice, I gave you time and now I'm gonna take what I'm owed." He shoves me backward and I flop onto the bed. Before I can move he's on top of me pinning my arms above my head.

"Get the fuck off me!" I scream hysterically as fear chokes me, I can't go through this again. He holds my wrists in one of his hands and uses his free hand to tear my shirt down, exposing my bra. "Darius is going to fucking kill you!" I scream right in his face. He doesn't use words, he silences me by punching me. Pain explodes in jaw, black spots dance in the corner of my eyes, and I pray that I pass out. I would rather be unconscious while he rapes me.

"You fucking cunt. I'm gonna destroy you. When I'm done fucking you, he won't take a second look." A sob tears out of me as he reaches between our bodies and pops the button on my cut-offs. Uncontrollable sobs continue to fall from me as he forces my shorts down my legs. I close my eyes, not wanting to witness him defile my body. Bile rises up my throat and I'm powerless to stop the vomit that forces it way out of me. I manage to turn my head at the last second as the contents of my breakfast messily lands on his bed. "Fucking bitch!" he snarls, grips the thin strap of my thong and rips it. A switch inside me flicks, I begin to scream and claw and fight with everything I have.

"Fuck you! Darius!" I scream over and over again. He

manages to land a few more hits to my face and body but I don't feel a thing. I continue to try to maim him anyway I can even when I hear the door kicked open. Everything happens within a second. I'm clawing at his face while he's punching me, then he's gone and I'm yanked off the bed. I see nothing but Garrett's face. I kick, scream and hit trying to break free. "Darius!" I scream so fucking loud my throat feels numb.

"Open your eyes, Goldie, I'm right here!" I trick myself into thinking I can hear his voice. "I'm here, baby, open your eyes. I'm right here!" I slowly blink my eyes open, the sight of his coffee-colored eyes is the first thing I see before I scream and throw myself at him. He arms band around me and hold me tightly against his chest. "I got you, Goldie." I can barely hear him over my own screams.

"Get her the fuck out of here," I hear my brother shout. I attempt to turn my head but Darius pushes my face into his chest.

"Beckett, give me your shirt," Darius grits out. I feel him shift a moment later. He tries to push me back but I won't let him. "Baby, I need to put this on you to… cover you." When he gently pushes me back a step, I allow an inch of space between us but no more, and my body begins to shake uncontrollably. Darius has a murderous look in his eyes. He gently pulls the shirt over my head. I hiss when the material scrapes my cheek. He curses beneath his breath as I push my arms through the holes, Beckett's shirt reaches past my knees. "I'm gonna carry–" Before he can finish, I launch myself at him, locking my arms and legs around him then bury my face in his neck. He pulls the shirt down over my ass and keeps one hand there while the other grips the back of my neck.

I can hear grunts and sounds of a struggle but I don't dare look. Darius walks us out of the room. I tighten my hold on him when we descend the stairs, even when I feel the sun on me I don't look up. I hear a car door open, but still I refuse to leave my hiding spot.

"You need to get in there. Crue and Beck are trying to pull him off that cunt," Darius growls.

"On it," I hear Saint say before the sound of his footfalls meet my ears.

"Goldie?" he says softly, when I don't move he sighs. "You gonna sit on my lap the whole way home?" I nod, a small chuckle escapes him as he maneuvers us in the car. "Baby, can you unlock your legs, we can't fit this way." I do as he says and shift so I'm sitting across his lap. I rest my sore face against his pec and stay silent. Neither of us say a word when the others return. Beckett slips into the driver's seat beside us, flicking his gaze to me and glowers.

"Let's go!" Corvin shouts from the back. Beck pulls his gaze from me and slams the car into gear before he drives away. Everyone is silent the whole way back to the guys' house. Beck kills the engine and no one makes a move to exit the car. I can't stop the tears from falling, quiet sobs continue to work their way out of me as I cling to Darius.

"If we don't get out, they're coming in." I flick my gaze up to see my friends standing at the bottom of the porch steps. Crue's right, the looks on their faces tell me we have mere seconds to decide before this car becomes overcrowded. I sit forward on Darius's lap and swivel around so I can see out the windscreen. A small hiss escapes me, my side is burning and it hurts to breathe. I think he may have fractured one of my ribs.

"Beckett, take Darius and Leah inside." I spy Beck nodding his agreement to Corv's order out of the corner of my eye. Darius shifts behind me and reaches over to open the door. I attempt to get out of the car but a whimper escapes me.

"Fuck!" Darius curses as he gently grips my arms and holds me in place. "Beck, get your ass over here and help her." Beckett rushes around to our side and offers me a hand with a warm smile, I take it. He and Darius help me out of the car. The second I stand on my own two feet, I feel like I am able to take a breath easier.

"Want me to carry you?" Beck asks. I shake my head and cringe when pain erupts in the side of my face. "Let's get you inside," he says as he wraps an arm around my waist leading me toward the house. I peer over my shoulder to see Corvin and Darius standing by the car staring at me. At the look of fury and pain on their faces I turn away. Cody and Katie stand there with tears trailing down their cheeks at the sight of me. Nathan rushes up to me, forcing us to a stop.

His eyes search mine for a second then he rushes past me toward the others. "I'm coming with you," he says. I don't have the energy to digest what they are up to. I smile at the girls, both of them stand there holding each other with heartache clear as day on their faces.

"You should see the other guy," I rasp out, trying to lighten the mood. It doesn't work, they both sob. Beck ushers me forward and up the porch steps, helps me inside and pauses in the living room.

"What do you need, babe?" he asks gently.

"A shower," I answer instantly. I need to scrub his touch from my skin. A shiver of disgust rolls through me.

"Okay, come on," he says quietly as he leads me to the stairs, helping me the whole way to the bathroom I shared with Darius. He releases his hold on me as he reaches into the stall and turns the shower on. I try to pull the shirt off but the pain in my side flares to life every time I move to lift my left arm. Beck steps in front of me and the distraught look on his face kills me. I don't even have the guts to look at the mirror. If I hurt this much I can only imagine what I must look like to them.

"Can you help me?" I ask, a whoosh of air escapes him as he nods. He grips the hem of his shirt and slowly pulls it over my head, when a growl escapes him I peer down at my body and flinch. My left side is bruised already, my thong is torn, hanging to one side exposing the top of my pussy. My shirt is hanging on by one thin piece, the strap on my bra is torn and scratch marks cover my body. Beck reaches out and tears my shirt. I shrug the material off and stand here before him in my ruined underwear.

"I'm so sorry, babe." The pain in his voice has me feeling the need to comfort him, I don't get the chance.

"I got it from here," Darius says as he comes to stand beside Beck. He runs his gaze over me, making me feel like I need to shield myself. I try to cover myself with my arms, but he isn't having that. He darts forward, and I flinch involuntarily when he reaches out to me. A horrified look crosses his face. "Goldie…" he breathes out my name brokenly.

"I'm sorry," I choke out, shaking my head. He slowly lifts his hands again to gently cup my face, careful not to apply too much pressure and cause me any more pain. He leans down resting his forehead against mine, I breathe him in trying to draw on what little strength I have inside me.

"Do you want me to help you get her in the shower?" Darius takes a shuddering breath as he slowly draws back but keeps his eyes on me.

"It's up to her." Darius answers quietly.

CHAPTER TWENTY

Darius

When she doesn't answer I try asking again. "Do you want Beck in here to help?" I can hear the strain in my own voice. I hated having to ask that but right now, I would give her anything she wanted. The fear in her eyes when I reached for her will haunt me for the rest of my life. She darts her tongue out to moisten her lips before flicking her eyes over my shoulder to Beckett. My heart drops, she would rather he help her than me.

"Becky, can you get me some water and painkillers, please?" I try to keep the surprise from my face.

"You got it, babe. I'll leave them on the side table in D's room," he says before he rushes off to do as she asks.

"Can you close the doors, please?" she asks quietly. I nod and do as she asked, closing and locking both doors before stepping in front of her again. I'm unsure of what the hell to do next. I fear with how angry I am, that if I touch her, I may cause her more harm. As if she can read my thoughts she speaks again. "Can you unhook my bra?" I nod and reach around her. She rests her forehead against my chest as I slowly push the straps down her arms, then kneel in front of her and slowly pull her ruined thong down her legs. I run my gaze along the inside of her thighs trying to spot any sign of bruising or… blood. "He never got the chance. I fought him, Darius," she cries. I stand in front of her, hating the broken look in her eyes. "I fucking fought him… I didn't… I wouldn't let…" Sobs wrack her tiny frame and I curse before throwing caution to wind.

I strip off and gently wrap my arm around her trembling form and usher her into the shower. I gently angle her under the spray and have to take several calming breaths when blood begins to cover the tiled floor. Her cheek is split, her eyebrow is cut. Her nose has crusted blood but it's not broken. Her bottom lip is covered in blood but no sign of a split. I gently run my hand through her hair, trying to get rid of the chunks in it. She reaches out and holds my waist letting me just comb my fingers through her hair.

"You're the strongest person I know, Goldie." She rests her head against my naked chest.

"I don't feel very strong." I gently lift her chin until her eyes are on mine, making sure she can see the seriousness in my eyes.

"You are, Leah. You have been through some fucked up shit and still you stand before me, unbroken and smiling. What Gary did to you…" I take a deep breath knowing this is overdue and needs to be said. "I should never have walked out on you that night. I allowed my trust issues from my past to bleed into what we shared. You needed me and I wasn't there. The things I did and said to you when you got here was fucked up." Fresh tears roll down her cheeks. "That night when that cunt played that tape, I should have been the one you came to, it should have been me that held you and helped you, not Beck. I'll never forgive myself for that, Goldie. I've fucked up a lot but I'm standing here before you asking you to give me one more chance, allow me to prove to you that I am worth it. Let me love you like I should have years ago."

"I want to believe you, I really do," she breathes out.

"Today, when shit went down you didn't call Beck or your brother, you called me. Why?" Her mouth opens but no words come so I push on. "You were screaming for *me*. You called my name, not Corvin's or Beckett's. Want to know why?" I don't give her a chance to answer. "Because deep down you know that no matter what I said or did to you, when you need me, I'll always be there. I'll always come when you call." It breaks me to say this but I know I have to. "If I've blown this and lost my chance, just tell me. I know Beck and you are close, it will flay me open to see you with him but—"

"I love, Becky," she cuts in, and my heart shatters inside my chest. I drop my gaze to the floor, unable to move or speak through the pain. "But not like you think." I snap my gaze back to hers. "Beck is like a... I don't know how to explain it but he's my Becky."

"And what am I?" I push.

"My everything," she whispers. My eyes search hers trying to see if she is lying but I see no sign of deceit.

"What does that mean, Goldie?" Her shoulders deflate.

"It means that I hate what you did to me and how you treated me but no matter how hard I tried, I couldn't hate you. I wanted so badly to just to stop the hurt I was feeling but I couldn't. I can never hate you because I love you too fucking much."

"You love me?"

"I've loved you since I was fourteen, Darius. I won't be your secret anymore, I can't." I brush my thumb along her bottom lip.

"I'll never hide you again. I swear just tell me you're mine."

"Only if you tell me the truth about everything?"

"Deal, now say it." She smiles then flinches, and I growl,

"Fuck, let's get you cleaned up and out of here, then into bed."

"I need to scrub his touch from my skin, can you help me?" I nod unable to speak for fear of losing the tiny grip I have on my temper. A part of me wishes I had gone with Corvin to finish the job, but I knew she needed me. Knowing that it was me she called and me she was screaming for had me turning down the offer and racing inside to be there for my girl. I'll never be able to unhear her screams. As I ran up the stairs of that frat house, hearing her screaming my name, I didn't think as I followed her screams, then kicked the door open. I froze for one second, then I was throwing that cunt off her. I didn't care about him, I just knew she needed me. Corvin and Crue beat the cunt and kept going even after he passed the fuck out. They gagged him and tied his ass up in his closet before they left. The three of them and Nathan have gone back to *dispose* of the evidence. Garrett will never be a problem again.

After making me scrub her twice and washing her hair she finally let me get her out of the shower. I dried her gently before dressing her in one of my shirts and putting her in my bed. She took the painkillers Beck left for her and five minutes later she was asleep. I sit here in the dark just watching her sleep. I'm unable to take my eyes off her for more than a second, guilt eats away at me for how I've treated her. I don't know what I would have done if that motherfucker raped her. I scrub my hands down my face trying to rid myself of those thoughts.

"I'm such a fuck up," I mutter to myself.

"Nah, man." I snap my gaze to the doorway to see Corvin standing there, the soft glow of the hall light casting him in a dark light. I look him over and slowly climb to my feet at the sight of blood on his shirt. He meets my stare as I step in front of him. His eyes are haunted and have a look in them I have never seen.

"What happened, Corv?" I ask softly.

"I did what I had to do." The conviction in which he says this has a pang of dread shooting down my spine. "Your brother's next." I furrow my brow.

"What?" His eyes harden, he reaches out and clutches my shirt in his hands.

"Gary told Garrett that my sister was fair game. That motherfucker thought he had a right to touch my sister because your brother told him she was *easy*." My eyes widen and my jaw slackens.

"When?" I ask.

"Garrett was the fucking witness, Darius! He was the one who caught Vic and Gary talking about what he did to Leah. Needless to say with that bastard suing you, that video of him admitting to what he did is long gone now!" I shake my head trying to deny what he is saying, that video was the key piece of evidence that we had to drop this case against us. I know this case against us is a big deal but the merger is complete, we have the money to back us. There isn't a thing Victor can do about that.

"I get it, Corvin, I do, but that shit has to wait. Right now, the only thing I care about is your sister and making sure she's okay." His face pulls taut, he uses his grip on my shirt to pull me closer leaving only a sliver of space between us.

"She comes first before everything in your life." I nod. "She didn't call me, Darius, she screamed for *you*, not me." The anguish I hear in his voice has me reaching out to grip the back of his neck and pushing my forehead against his.

"She called me because she knew no matter what happens between us, that I'll always come running. I put her through some fucked up shit and I have a lot to make up for."

"Yeah, you do." Comes from behind us. I tear out of

Corv's hold as I rush toward her. He flicks the light on before he joins us and sits on the opposite side of the bed. I perch on the edge of the bed and reach out to grip her hand in mine. Her face is busted up and bruised. I hate the pained look I see in her eyes, her vibrant green eyes have dulled.

"How you feeling?" Corv asks softly. She tries to smile reassuringly but it doesn't reach her eyes.

"Sore, but also glad to see you two not fighting." Corv and I both chuckle.

"He's a dick but… seeing what he went through to get to you today showed me, I have to get over my hang up on you two… being together." Leah's face is a picture of surprise. "You two are together, right?" he asks as he looks between me and her.

"Yes."

"No," we answer in unison. I narrow my eyes at her.

"The fuck do you mean *no*?" I grit out. I ignore Corvin as he whistles between his teeth. Leah's face is blank as she stares at me. "We talked this shit out in the shower!" I growl.

"Fuck me!" Corvin grounds out but we ignore him.

"I told you, I want the truth and until I get that, no, we're not together." I take some deep breaths through my nose to try calm my anger.

"It's not just his story to tell," Corvin answers for me. "You want answers about why we started our business then you need to hear it from all of us, but only when you're better." She nods. "Do you really want to know?"

"About your business or about the blood that is covering your hands and clothes?" she retorts, causing Corv to flinch. "Look, if it's something you guys don't want to share then that's fine, I get it."

Fuck this. "Everyone has their own reasons for wanting to start this, mine is a lot more petty than the others," I answer. She searches my gaze trying to find any sign of deceit, which she won't.

"Okay." I frown.

"What does that mean, Goldie." She shrugs.

"It means, I'll wait for you to tell me when you're ready." I nod, I may be reading between the lines here but I feel like there is a double meaning to what she's saying.

"Thank you?" It comes out more like a question than I want it to.

"So, now that we have that sorted, can I pee and go to the spare room?" My eyes snap wide.

"What?" I cringe at how loud I say that, the little devil just smiles at me.

"Well, we're not together and it would be wrong for me to share your bed." Corvin's laughter just pisses me off, the fucker isn't going to be laughing in a second.

"We weren't together while Corvin was away at camp and you sure as shit didn't fucking mind staying in *my* bed then." Corvin leaps off the bed like it burnt him, laughter tears from me at the disgusted look on his face.

"Fuck you! Get the fuck out. My sister doesn't like you and needs to pee." I lull my head toward him and smirk as I say.

"So, you gonna help her out of her thong so she can pee…" I let my sentence trail off, and the glare he shoots my way has me shaking with silent laughter.

"Millions of people in the world and she chooses you!" He looks back to Leah with a hopeful look in his eyes. "I'll find you someone else, anyone else, just not this prick." Laughter bursts from Leah before she hisses and grips her left side in pain. Corvin and I are on her in a second.

"Call the doc," I snap.

"On it," he says as he races from the room to do as I asked. I reach out and brush her hair back from her face, hating that I can't take her pain away.

CHAPTER TWENTY-ONE

Leah

Darius insisted he be the one to help me pee. I have never been more mortified in my life than having him help me. He never commented once, even though shame burned through me. He stayed by my side the whole time as the doctor checked me out. I have bruised ribs which should heal in a couple weeks, nothing broken in my face, just badly bruised. I nearly died of shame when the doctor told me I would need to wait at least a week before resuming sexual activities.

"I'm so sorry I wasn't there, we should have come with you." I clasp Katie's hand in mine and smile. Her, Cody and Nathan barged in the second the doctor, Corvin and Darius went into the hall to *talk*.

"This isn't your fault," I tell her.

"I fucking hate that dog shit bastard." My eyes widen at Cody's outburst.

"He won't be hurting you or anyone else ever again." I turn to look at Nathan who is leaning against the wall across from me. He doesn't have his usual… spunk on display, he looks weighed down.

"What does that mean?" I ask hesitantly. He sighs before running a hand through his blonde hair, his green eyes are hollow and plagued. I hate seeing that look on him. He tears his gaze from me to stare out the window, ignoring my question. I decide to let it go, I don't need more shit to deal with on top of everything else.

"So, you and Darius, huh?" Cody teases. I shake my head causing a frown to mar her beautiful face.

"We're just... friends," I answer. A snort comes from Nathan, drawing our attention to him.

"Baby, no *friends* look at each other the way you two do and trust me, that man stares at you with hunger." His words have a fire stirring in my belly. "From what I heard, Mr. tall dark and handsome sure as fuck doesn't want to be friends."

"Who told you that?" He shoots me a dry stare.

"He told Beckett that if he ever touched you again he would break his arms and make it look like an accident." I gasp, what the fuck! "Want my advice?"

"Uh, sure?" I answer warily.

"Get out of your own way and stop denying what is inevitable. You two are cosmic. That type of love happens once in a lifetime, don't blow it." His words hit me hard as I hear the truth in them. I know he's right but I just need time.

The pain in my side rouses me awake, I cringe when I shift slightly then freeze when I feel something pressed against my back. I peer over my shoulder and roll my eyes at the sight of Darius asleep behind me. I kept my word and slept in the spare room, the girls and Nathan said they would stay with me. Darius was pissed but didn't argue, now I get why he didn't. He never planned to sleep in his own bed. I slowly edge myself out of the bed and sit up slowly so I don't aggravate the pain in my side. Swinging my legs over the side of the bed, I stifle my gasp.

My heart burst inside my chest, laying there on the floor

beside me on a mattress is a sleeping Beck. I carefully stand and make sure not to step on him as I try to make my way out of the room. I freeze when I reach the end of the bed, my friends did sleep in here just not alone. Katie is sandwiched between Crue and Saint, Corvin is wrapped around Cody as they sleep. I spy Nathan's feet peeking out from the other side of the bed, and a smile breaks free. I am so fucking lucky to have these amazing people in my life. I am honestly so blessed. I slowly make my way through to the bathroom and out Darius's open bedroom so I don't wake anyone using my bedroom door.

It takes me an age to get down the stairs, but I manage. As soon as I enter the kitchen, I flick the coffee pot on before grabbing some of the pain pills from the drawer. I down two with a glass of water, praying they will kick in soon. My face is tender and achy today, the doctor said that was to be expected. Getting punched in the face from Gary was a walk in the park compared to this. I pour myself a cup of coffee once it's ready and decide to head out the back and enjoy the crisp morning air. It's going to be too cold soon to be out here, so I want to enjoy it while I can.

I slowly lower myself into one of the loungers, I snag the throw blanket off the other chair and wrap it around my legs before reclining back and sipping my coffee. I sit here silently reflecting on the events of yesterday. They were horrific and will take me time to get over, but if those events didn't occur would Darius have had the balls to tell me how he really feels?

"I planned to tell you yesterday." I startle at the sound of his voice. I lean forward and shoot him a dirty look for scaring me.

"Tell me what?" He pins me with a *really* look before coming over. He doesn't ask or even see if I mind, he just hops in behind me and settles me between his legs, caging my own between his.

"You were thinking out loud again, now lean back and share that blanket." I sigh but do as he says. I'll admit this is much more comfy leaning on him than the plastic of the chair. He absentmindedly runs his fingers up and down my arms as I sip my coffee. "Why are you up so early?"

"You wouldn't know I was up this early if you were in your own bed," I sassily reply. He laughs lightly, leans down and places a kiss to my cheek, before whispering in my ear.

"Get used to it, because you're moving in with me." The feeling of his lips scraping against the shell of my ear almost has me distracted enough to not comprehend his words —almost.

"I'm not moving in with you," I say firmly.

"Fine, you want the truth, Leah? I'll give it to you but once I do tell you, you better give up this whole bullshit."

"What bullshit?" I snap.

"The next time you tell someone we are just *friends*, I'll fuck you right there in front of them just so they know how *friendly* we really are!" His words should piss me off, but all they do is turn me the fuck on. Something is seriously wrong with me.

"You heard that, huh?" I ask, trying my hardest to not laugh.

"I mean it, you're mine, Leah, and I'm tired of lying to myself and everyone else about it. I let you go once and I won't be dumb enough to do it a second time." His words have my heart soaring.

"What about Corvin?"

"He knows how I feel about you and even if he isn't good with it, I made my choice, Goldie."

I dart my tongue out to moisten my lips. "What did you choose?" I ask quietly. He wraps his arms around me gently and buries his face into the crook of my neck, where he places an open-mouthed kiss.

"I picked the right sibling this time." Tears prick the backs of my eyes. "I'll never make you doubt your importance to me again. You'll always be my first choice, Leah."

"Tell me the truth and I'll give you my answer." He snorts.

"I'll just fuck a yes out of you but whatever helps you feel like you're in control, for now." I balk at his boldness. "Here we go. Once upon a time." I can't stop the laugh that breaks free and immediately regret it when the pain in my side flares to life. "No laughing or I stop." I nod. "Okay, so you know about my mom and me moving in with you guys." I nod. "Okay, well I lied to you. I found out who my dad was when I was twelve. My mom let it slip in one of her episodes about him and how he took the good twin. I didn't believe her at first until I did some digging."

"Did Corvin know?" I feel him nod behind me.

"Yeah, he knew. He helped me get the records of my birth. I hadn't planned to do anything at that time, it wasn't until we met Saint, Crue and Beckett that we came up with a plan."

"Why?" I ask still unable to piece all the dots together myself.

"Saint would go on about how he hated his father and what he did. He didn't tell us why until one night we all got drunk. I spilled about who my father was, and that was when Saint came clean. Honestly, the only ones with a vendetta are me and Saint. Crue, Beck and Corvin are doing this to help their families and support us as well, but also set themselves up with a great future."

"What did Saint say?"

"He said that his dad knew Victor and that they did shady dealings together. He went on to tell us about his dad's tech company and how he made an app. This app wasn't like any of the others he had ever made before. To get this app you had to pay a hundred grand."

"For what exactly?" I can feel this story is about to take a dark turn.

"This app is used to distribute any information. You can

post videos that can't be traced, download illegal content of children." I gasp, horrified at what he is saying. "You see, Victor is a sick fuck and he used his hotels and resorts to film children. Devon sold the content on his app. This made them both millions. We decided there and then that we would do whatever it took to take down mine and Saint's father. We worked our asses off, studied the stock market and learned how to invest. We didn't have the money, so we started out small and truthfully, we got a lucky break that made us the money we needed to expand. We kept expanding until we had enough money to buy Victor's company that has been in his family for generations–still is, I guess. He has a gambling problem and was in debt up to his eyeballs. He had to either sell or go bankrupt, needless to say when we put in the offer he jumped at it."

"I don't know what to say, I had no idea." I feel so disgusted and heartbroken for those poor children that were used.

"There isn't anything to say. With Katie helping us now, we are so much closer to being able to take Devon down. Saint is planning a hostile takeover with the board of Devon's company as soon as he has the proof."

"Then what?"

"Then Saint is selling the company. He wants nothing to do with his father's empire. His dad has tried to blackmail him for years and get him to give up his dream of being drafted and go work for him." I sit here silently for a long moment trying to digest what he's told me.

"What about Gary suing you?" I ask.

"He can try. We have the money this time and he doesn't. His daddy is broke. We'll hold him up in legal paperwork until he runs out of money. This is his last ditched effort to try and one up me. He'll never get the upper hand, we made sure of that." A shiver runs through me at his words, they sound so final.

CHAPTER TWENTY-TWO

Darius

I start to get worried when she says nothing for a long time. I know I just laid shit out for her but if telling her the truth means I get my girl, then I have no regrets.

"Gary used me to get to you, didn't he?"

"Yeah, Goldie."

"Did Gary know about you being his twin?" I shake my head even though she can't see me.

"No, he hated me and Corvin because of football. He had no idea that we were even related at that time. Gary is fucked up, Goldie." She snorts.

"Yeah, I'm well aware of that fact."

"Gary knew my mom sold her body for drugs. After what he did to you, he tried to *buy* my mom." She gasps and slowly turns sideways so she can face me, her face a picture of disgust.

"He tried to sleep with his own mother?" I roll my lips over my teeth and nod. "Oh, that is just gross."

"Yeah, it is," I admit.

"Did he… do it?"

"No."

"Thank God—"

"It wasn't from his lack of trying. But, apparently even Jenny Lockhart has a moral compass and draws the line at fucking her own son," I say with an edge to my voice.

"Wait, so your mom knew who Gary was the whole time?" I grit my teeth and nod, her eyes soften. "How?"

I take a deep breath before giving her the story she eagerly wants. "When Gary and I turned one, Victor turned up at the trailer park demanding one of us."

"Why?" I hear tinges of pain in her voice, but it isn't for herself, it's for me.

"Victor's father told him that he wouldn't hand over the company to him unless he had an heir that he could pass the company onto." Anger flares to life in her eyes.

"Victor never wanted Gary, he just wanted to inherit his fortune." I nod. "How did he know your mom?"

"Jenny said she met him at a bar she used to sing at, some swanky joint in the city. He would screw her every time he was in town. She got knocked up and Victor fled, leaving her alone and pregnant. She lost her job and had no choice but to move out of the city into a trailer park where she raised us for a year, until Victor came and stole Gary." Her eyes widen and her mouth pinches to the side. I can see the cogs of her mind turning over. "Just say it."

"When did your mom start doing drugs and... prostituting herself?" I frown.

"Why?" She reaches out and cups my face between her hands, sadness clouds her features.

"Just answer, please." I try to think back to when I first remember her starting to dabble in narcotics.

"Maybe around the time I turned two. She didn't shoot up at first, she just started to drink. Then, when that didn't give her a buzz, she started on the hard shit and well, you know the rest."

"Oh, Darius," she says brokenly. I lean forward and gently grip her waist as I place a soft kiss to her lips.

"Don't pity me, baby. Look at me now," I say in a light tone, trying to ease some of the tension. She shakes her head.

"Darius, you don't get it, do you?"

I furrow my brow, not picking up what she is putting down. "Get what, Goldie?" I ask, slightly exasperated and over this whole conversation. Dragging up the past does nothing. All it ever does is make me hate Jenny and Victor more for not loving me like the Williams's love their children.

"Darius, your mom turned to drinking and drugs because she was broken hearted."

"What?" I practically shout.

"Did she willingly hand Gary over?" I scrunch my face up as I try to remember that day. I can't, all I know is what she told me.

"She said she hated Victor because he took her purpose away. I... I don't think she gave him up, I think Victor just... took him."

"Your mom was trying to dull her pain through alcohol and drugs, Darius." I cock my head to the side and stare at her, trying to process her words. "The day you moved in with us, what did your mom say?" I scoff.

"The bitch packed my shit for me," I bite out.

"So, she said nothing else to you?" I roll my eyes and try to think back to that day. I remember the Williams's calling her and her agreeing to let me live with them. When we drove to the trailer park, I went and grabbed my bags and then—my eyes widen.

"She told me... that your parents could give me a better life. She said sorry and... cried." My stomach drops and a lump forms in my throat. Holy fuck. Is Leah right? Did my mom actually love me?

"Darius?" she whispers my name, trying to draw my gaze back to her. When I take too long, she grips my chin and lifts my face to hers. Her eyes are filled with pity and it causes me to flinch.

"I don't need your pity," I snarl. She doesn't pull away or reprimand me for my harsh tone.

"I don't pity you, babe. I pity Jenny for what she went through." Is it wrong that the only thing I heard out of what she just said was *babe*?

I smirk. "Babe, huh?" She rolls her eyes.

"I'm serious," she says sternly.

"What do you want me to say? It's too late now. I'm not a little kid anymore, Goldie. I gave up hope a long time ago."

"It's never too late. If you want to find her, I'll help you and be there with you every step of the way. I promise!" I mull over her words. What if she's right and Jenny really was just fucked up and trying to ease the pain of losing a child? She didn't have the money to fight Victor and she was dumb enough to put his name on our birth certificates, so it's not like he was kidnapping in a way and knowing Victor, he would have threatened her to not go to the cops.

"I'll… think about it." Before we can discuss this any further, the back door opens and a pale looking Crue stands there. "What's wrong?"

"We have a problem." The solemn tone of his voice has us both climbing to our feet. I help Leah and then lead her inside where we find the others sitting in the living room with news playing on the TV.

'The remains of college student Garrett Jones has been found near the local park. It appears that this wasn't from natural causes and the police are treating this as a homicide. Anyone with information is urged to come forward–

Corvin turns the TV off before the rest can be heard. No one says a word. We all stand around, reeling over what we just heard. My first thought is thank fuck the cunt is dead and the second, what the fuck did Corvin and the others do?

"What did you do?" Leah breathes out as she looks at her brother. Corvin doesn't look broken up or even worried. He cuts his gaze to Cody and Katie, both the girls look to be in shock. His gaze hardens as he continues to stare at Cody, daring her to say something. She swallows audibly before standing on shaky legs, she squares her shoulders and lifts her chin as she meets Corvin's harsh stare.

"We know nothing. We came over yesterday to continue the celebrations from the Thanksgiving party and everyone was here the *whole* night." Corvin pulls his gaze from Cody to look at Katie. Unlike Cody, her gaze is fixated on the two guys standing beside Corvin. Crue and Saint have a mask of indifference in place, keeping their emotions locked down. She pushes to her feet and ignores Corvin as she stands before the duo. Those two boys would die for each other, there is nothing and no one in this world that could ever come between them. If Katie has any hope of making it a trio, her answer better be the same as Cody's.

"Whatever you need me to say, I'll say it. I won't lie, I'm not sad that asshole is dead and if that makes me a shitty person, so be it." The tension drains from Saint's shoulders. Crue grips Katie's face and plasterers his mouth to hers. Well, clearly that was the right answer after all. I look to Corvin to find his gaze already on me, I see it. I can read him better than anyone, they did it. They killed Garrett.

After setting Leah up in the living room with Cody and Katie, the five of us and Nathan make our way to the basement. Once we're inside, Crue closes the door while Saint sets his phone up to the Bluetooth speaker, no one speaks until the music begins to play.

"What happened last night?" I ask as I look between Nathan, Crue, Saint and Corvin. I'll admit I'm shocked as fuck that Nathan was a part of this, we never do any dodgy shit with someone else around only each other.

"It's not what you think," Crue begins but Corvin cuts him off.

"We got back there, the fucker was dead in the closet. What the fuck were we supposed to do?"

"He was breathing when we left," Beck interjects. Corvin just shrugs his shoulders.

"Well, he wasn't when we got back." Corvin forgets I can read him, I know he's lying but the thing I don't get is why? "We disposed of the body and made sure nothing would link back to us."

"The whole fucking house saw us running through there to get to Leah!" I rebuke.

"They're taken care of," Saint answers.

"How?" Saint's mask falters, I stare at him for a second as I try to piece this all together. How the hell would they have got a whole fucking house to remain silent and not snitch about a murder?

"Look, we did what we had to," Crue says in a matter of fact tone.

"And what about him?" I ask as I nod my head toward Nathan, he glares at me.

"Well I won't be saying shit, will I?" he snaps.

"We're just supposed to believe that?" Beck asks.

"Asshole over there snapped a pic of me carrying the body, so I'd say I'm good at keeping my mouth shut." Corvin nods his agreement, this shit is too much to deal with.

"All of you get your clothes from last night and burn them now, all the bedding you slept in needs to be burned. Whatever car you took needs to be detailed stat. You need Katie to hack into any cameras around the area that you went to and scrub the footage. We all need to get our story about yesterday straight and come up with a damn good lie about Leah's face."

"Since when did you become a pro on covering up a murder?" Saint jokes.

"Since this isn't my first cover up," Beckett answers in a flat tone, he marches out of the room as the rest of us stare at his retreating form, stunned.

"He wasn't joking, was he?" Crue whispers. I shake my head.

"I think there is still a shit load we don't know about Beck and something tells me, he was telling the truth just then," I utter.

We come up with a plan that the girls and Nathan will stay with us for the rest of the break, that way if the cops come knocking, we'll all be together. Saint and Crue left an hour ago with Katie to go back to the dorms to pack them some shit. Nathan left not long after them to go grab some shit for himself.

"This is so not how I envisioned my homecoming to be," Leah mumbles. I wrap my arm around her shoulders, she rests her head on my chest. Corv and Cody sit on the sofa opposite us while Beck sits on the bean bag near the fireplace stoking it, burning the clothes and bedding.

"Me either," Cody answers, shooting her friend a rueful smile.

"How did you picture it?" I ask.

"I can't answer that with my brother in the same room." I splutter as Corvin shoots Leah a scathing look.

"That shit isn't funny," Corv snaps. He's been in a salty mood since Cody said she would be staying in the spare room. Beck offered up his room to Nathan, so of course Leah had to then offer him to crash with us in *my bed*.

"It was a little funny," she teases. I shake my head at the pair of them. "Becky?" she calls. Beckett slowly turns to face her, he smiles but it's forced. "You okay?"

"Yeah, babe, just thinking." I hate that he fucking calls her stupid ass pet names, it works on my nerves. The front door opens to reveal Crue, Saint and Katie. I narrow my eyes.

Katie's cheeks are flushed, her hair is a mess and Crue's shirt is on backwards.

"So, campus is like a five minute drive and by my calculations, you guys have been gone over an hour?" Katie shoots Cody a dirty look before dropping the bag in her hand to the floor.

"Whoops," she hisses as she stares at Cody.

"Bitch, you better not have broken my GHD," Cody mumbles as she slouches back into the couch. Fuck me, I can tell I'm already going to regret having them all stay with us.

CHAPTER TWENTY-THREE

One week…

It's been a week since *that* day. None of us have left the house and I'm starting to go stir crazy! Darius is constantly hovering making sure I'm okay, Nathan and Saint are always bickering. Cody and Corvin fight nonstop all day which means we all have to listen to them fuck nightly. That's not the worst part, once Cody starts screaming, Crue and Saint make it their life mission to make Katie scream louder! Beck kicked Nathan out of his room and put him in the room next to Darius and me since Cody never sleeps in it. I'm glad my girls are getting– well I'm glad Katie is but it grosses me out to think about Cody and my brother. My ribs are fine now and my face doesn't ache, the bruising makes it look worse than it is. I've tried for the past two nights to get Darius to touch me but he won't, and it's fucking killing me!

I need something to help ease the stress. I'm walking around a house with five hot as fuck guys, Cody says it's six guys but eww, the sixth doesn't count because he's my brother! These guys barely wear clothes, they prance around shirtless all day. Some days they don't even wear shorts and just walk around in their boxers. I can't help it, no matter how hard I try my eyes always seem to stray to their cocks and fuck me, I already know Darius and Beck are *huge*, but I can't miss the bulges in the other two's pants.

"Goldie!" Darius snaps. I dart my gaze to him to find him pinning me with a murderous glare. "I'm sitting right fucking here!" I throw my hands up as I push back from the table. I place my hands on it and lean over slightly, narrowing my eyes.

"Maybe I wouldn't be caught staring at their dicks daily if you actually let me see *yours!*" I yell. I can feel the others staring at us but I don't care, there is no such thing as privacy in this house anyway.

"Leah!" Corvin shouts behind me. I ignore him as I watch Darius slowly stand from his chair opposite me and mimic my stance. His eyes burn with lust, that look has heat spreading throughout my body.

"You want me to fuck you?" he asks huskily.

"Yes!" I shout.

"No!" Corvin and I both answer in unison. I grit my teeth as I spin around to find Corvin being blocked in the kitchen by Katie, Beck and Crue. I spy Nathan and Cody out of the corner of my eye watching us from over the back of the sofa. Saint still sits next to Darius eating his sandwich.

"So, you get to fuck every night while we all have to listen but I can't?" I grind out.

"Yes," Corvin answers, which just pisses me off.

"Uh, no, that does not work for me!" My brother narrows his eyes in warning.

"I don't care. That shit is not happening while I'm in the house–"

"Then get a fucking hotel!" I shout. I hear Darius and Saint laugh behind me, I even see Crue and Beck shake with silent laughter. Corvin's face turns red, he looks like he is about to blow a blood vessel in his forehead.

"You know they have slept together before, right?" Saint quips.

"Not while I've been around!" he answers cockily. I smirk and tilt my chin up as I say,

"Are you sure?" Darius chokes on something behind me as Corvin's mouth drops open. He darts his gaze over my head to Darius.

"She's full of shit…right?" The pleading in Corvin's voice nearly has me curling over and laughing.

"Y-yeah?" Darius stutters.

"Why the fuck did that sound like a lie?" Corvin shouts.

I throw my hands in the air. "Because it was. I gave him a blow job on the couch at home while you were passed out on the other chair. He also snuck into my room most nights, oh and we also fucked in your shower at home." He turns pale and hunches over gripping the edge of the counter. Darius is cursing beneath his breath behind me. I turn around and pin him with a stern look that has him standing up straight. "Just in case you didn't get the point, you either start putting out or I'm moving in with–"

"Swear to fucking God, if you say Beckett…" Darius warns. I scrunch my face up.

"I was gonna say Nathan," I answer. The tension eases from his shoulders.

"Why would it matter if she stayed with Beck?" Nathan fails at whispering to Cody. I roll my lips over my teeth to stop from smiling which earns me a scornful look from Darius.

"I need a fucking drink," Corvin grumbles behind me. An idea hits me as Darius eyes me warily.

"Why are you looking at me like that?" he asks suspiciously.

"We're about to play a drinking game that guarantees I get laid!" I say nodding, pleased with myself.

"You don't even care about me!" I whine as he holds my hair while I wash my face in the bathroom sink.

"Goldie, I have held your hair back while you threw up, helped shower and change you, brushed your teeth and here I am currently still holding your freaking hair back. How the hell is that me not caring about you?" I ponder that for a second, my mind is fuzzy from the alcohol I consumed. I thought it would be a great idea to challenge the guys to a drinking game hoping to get Darius drunk enough that I could seduce him. Turns out all the guys and Nathan are pros at beer pong. I thought us three girls playing in swimsuits would throw them off their game. What a stupid idea that was.

"You haven't even asked me if I'm okay." I pout as I meet his gaze in the mirror. He rolls his eyes heavenward and takes a deep breath, almost like he is praying for patience.

He flicks his eyes back to mine and asks, "Are you okay?"

"No!" I practically shout and stomp my foot like a child.

"For the love of fucking Christ, what's wrong now?" he asks. I spin around and lean against the sink as I try my hardest to look sexy.

"I hurt," I say in the best sad voice I can muster.

"Where?" I keep the smirk off my face as I reach out, grab his hand and place it flat against my pussy.

"Right, here." His eyes darken, a small groan slips from his lips as he closes his eyes.

"We can't." His voice is pained. I can see from how stiff his shoulders are and the way his breathing has picked up that he's close to giving in.

"Why? You said you would do *anything* to make me feel better." He slowly lifts his eyes to meet mine. I can see a war inside them, he wants me but he's holding back. I don't want to give him too much time to think, so I release my hold on his hand–which he leaves against my pussy—grab the hem of my shirt and slowly pull it over my head. Chucking it to the side, his eyes drop to my exposed tits. I grip the waistband of my booty shorts and push them down, forcing his hand away as I do. I stand here naked and ready for him to take me, but he still won't make a move.

The buzz from the alcohol is still there so I decide to embrace it and allow my inner temptress out. I push up onto the counter and scoot back until my back is against the mirror. His gaze runs over me sending a trail of heat through my body. The hunger in his eyes is what gives me the courage to make my next move. I open my legs, bending them at the knee to balance on the edge of the counter. His eyes drop to my exposed pussy. I bite my bottom lip as I slowly trail my hand down my chest and stop when I reach the apex of my thighs. Darius clenches his hands into fists at his sides, he's shaking, trying so hard to not give into his need. That's fine, I'm no quitter and I plan to have him inside me tonight no matter what it takes. I slip a finger through my folds and gasp.

"Stop…that's, you—fuck!" I smirk at his inability to form a coherent sentence. I push a finger inside my tight, wet hole, moaning his name as I do it. "Ah fuck," he grits out. I continue to pump that finger in and out of myself a couple times before switching to circling my clit.

"Oh my God," I breathe out as I arch my back off the mirror. "Yes!" I moan.

"Fuck it!" he growls before my hand is smacked out of the way. I smirk when he scowls at me.

"If you won't make me come then I have no choice but to take care of my own needs." He pushes forward until he stands between my legs, he bends his head down and ghosts his lips over mine as he says,

"I'm the only one who will be taking care of your needs, baby, no one else." He smashes his lips against mine. I open for him like always. I try to deepen the kiss but he jerks back like I just burned him.

"What the fuck?" I shout. He shoots me a pleading look, urging me to understand but I don't. "Why won't you fucking touch me?" I gasp as it begins to dawn on me. "Oh my God…" I push off the counter and quickly grab my clothes before racing into our room and trying to find my bag to pack my stuff and leave.

"What the hell are you doing?" he asks as I start toward the closet to grab my things. He blocks my path but I can't meet his stare.

"Let me go," I snap as he grips my arms holding me still.

"Not until you tell me what the fuck is going on?" I drop my chin to my chest.

"You should have told me." I hear the watery tone of my own voice.

"Told you what?" I shove him against his chest, causing him to stumble back a step. Not giving a shit that I'm standing here butt naked, I place my hands on my hips and hold his angry gaze.

"If knowing about Gary and what happened with Garrett has… put you off me, then you should have said something!" I latch onto my anger so I don't cry, his face drops.

"The fuck, Leah?" I flinch at the anger in his voice. He eliminates the space between us, gripping the back of my neck in a punishing grip as he pulls me toward him. I try to shake free but he uses his other arm to wind around my waist and hold me flush against him.

"Let. Me. Go," I snarl. He pushes his face against mine, not trying to mask the fury in his gaze.

"Shut the fuck up!" I keep the surprise off my face at how angry he is. "You think that the sight of you turns me off?" He thrusts his hips forward forcing me to feel his hard cock against my stomach. "Does that feel like the sight of you disgusts me?" he grits out.

"Then...why?" I ask.

"Because I didn't want you think I was fucking pressuring you after everything you have been through. I wouldn't blame you if the idea of sex put you off. But you couldn't let me be the nice guy, could you?" I open my mouth to answer but no words come out. "Close your fucking mouth or I'm putting my cock in it and I'll show you just how much the thought of fucking you disgusts me." I'm a wanton mess. I can feel the slickness between my thighs, my nipples hard and begging for his touch.

"Do it," I taunt. A sinister look enters his eyes before he darts his tongue out to lick my lips.

"You tempt me, but not tonight." My face falls. "I'll shove my cock down your throat tomorrow. Tonight, I'm gonna fuck you and show you just how much the sight of you makes me crazy and forces me to lose control. There is nothing about you that I don't love." I can't even process his words before his mouth is on mine, he doesn't hold back this time. This kiss isn't rushed or forced, it's him pouring all his feelings into it and showing me without words that he loves me. I wrap my arms around his neck, needing him closer. He moves his hands down my body leaving goosebumps in his wake as he grips the backs of my legs and lifts me. I break the kiss as I stare down at him, I see nothing but love and raw need for me in his eyes. "I love you, Leah, don't ever doubt that."

My brows draw in at his words, my heart takes flight inside my chest. "I love you too, now show me how much you want me," I taunt. A dark smirk crosses his face, forcing me to quirk a brow in question.

"I plan to make you scream all night long. You ready for the silent treatment from your brother tomorrow?" I cringe and screw my face up in disgust.

"Don't ever, and I mean ever, mention my brother when I'm naked and begging you to fuck me." He laughs as he walks us back toward the bed and lowers me down gently. He stands there between my legs, looking down at me for a minute before he trails his fingers up the top of my thighs and along my stomach. The closer he gets to my tits makes me fight the shivers that want to break free. At the last second, he skims his hands around the sides missing my nipples and drawing a pained whimper from me.

"What's wrong, baby?" he asks, teasingly, as he skates his hands down the same path. He may have said everything right but I can tell from the way his touch is unsure that he still thinks I'm not ready for this.

"Darius?" His eyes slowly lift to mine. "I'm not made of glass, you won't break me." He cocks his head to the side, frowning. "I want this, I want *you* to wipe away the bad and replace it with the good. Can you do that?" He searches my face for a sign of me being unsure, he won't find that. This isn't just about sex, this is about me needing to feel close to him again and reconnecting us in the most intimate way.

CHAPTER TWENTY-FOUR

Darius

I push my shorts down my legs, allowing my cock to spring free. Immediately her eyes zero in on it. It's been driving me crazy watching her check out the guys all week, jealousy reared its ugly head when I would find her staring at Beck. I've held myself back from touching her because I was scared that I would scare her or cause her to have a flashback. She didn't make it fucking easy! Tonight, the little show she put on nearly had me going crazy watching her prance around in that little yellow two-piece that barely covered anything.

I move forward and slowly lower myself on top of her, placing my hands on either side of her head before slowly lowering to my elbows. We've had sex plenty of times but the last time wasn't good between us. I need to make up for that. She rakes her nails down my back sending a shiver trailing down my spine and has a proud smile gracing her beautiful face. I kiss her, loving the way one kiss from me has her melting. I grind my cock into her, forcing a gasp from her. I refuse to allow her to break the kiss, swallowing her moan when I do it again. I can feel her arousal all over my cock as I slide it through her folds. She whimpers into my mouth and digs her nails into my sides. I relish in the pain.

I allow her to break the kiss. "Please." The way she says that one word with so much necessity has me caving and abandoning my plans on drawing this out and making her beg. I grip her face between my hands and splay my fingers wide, brushing the tops of my thumbs over her lips, then I slowly ease inside her. The second the head of my cock breaches her entrance her eyes begin to glaze over. I keep pushing inside her slowly, wanting to savor this moment and the feeling of being inside her. It's a feeling I'll never take for granted again.

I thrust in and out of her slowly while maintaining eye contact the entire time. I've never wanted to look at anyone but her while having sex. I love the way her mouth parts as a small moan slips free or the way her eyes turn glassy when I hit that sweet spot inside her. I just love looking at her, knowing that I'm the one bringing her this pleasure. I'm the only one who gets to bring her to this apex of a high that has her breaking apart beneath me, yet trusting me enough to allow me to do it.

"Darius, just like that." Her voice is raspy, her face slightly scrunched as I continue to push in and out of her, loving the way her pussy grips my cock, trying to keep me inside her. "I need more," she cries. I release my hold on her face as I grip her under her arms and pull her up as I rest back on my haunches. She lowers slowly down on my cock moaning. She runs her fingers through my hair before kissing me. I run my hands down her back, gripping the globes of her ass in my hands. She moans into my mouth and I pull my hand back and spank her ass. She jolts in my hold. Her eyes are wide with shock, but before she can think too much, I do it again but this time she cries out in pleasure. Fuck.

I grip her ass and hold her in place as I fuck her. I tried to give her slow and passionate but that's just not us. Leah and I love to fuck. She loves it hard, rough and dirty, just like me. The harder I slam inside her the louder her cries grow. She locks her arms around my neck as she throws her head back, screaming. I lean forward and bite down on the soft flesh between her neck and shoulder, sucking it into my mouth making sure to leave my mark on her.

"Oh my God, don't stop!" she screams. I know without a doubt everyone in the house can hear her and I fucking love them knowing that she's mine and it's my cock she's about to come on.

"Come for me, Goldie," I grit out. My command is her undoing.

"Darius!" she cries out as her pussy walls clamp down on my cock, and shudders roll through her. I'm too far gone to bring her down gently. I slam inside her harder than before, chasing my own release. I continue to pound in and out of her, loving the screams that tear out of her. She slams her mouth against mine, swallowing my moans and as I come inside her, a tremor races through my body the moment I stop moving. She breaks the kiss, resting her forehead against mine. We're both breathing fast and coated in a sheen of sweat. "We are so back together, just in case that wasn't clear."

I laugh then plant a quick peck to her lips before turning us and lying flat on my back with her on top and my cock still inside her. "We were always back together." She leans forward and crosses her arms over my chest before resting her chin atop them and staring down at me. I wrap my arms around her back and hold her here.

"You chased my buzz away," she says, then giggles. I'll never tire of hearing the sound of her laughter.

"You gave me a buzz." She rolls her eyes.

"Bet you say that to all the girls," she jokes.

"Nah, baby, only you. There was never anyone else for me but you." Her face softens.

"So, does that mean I can officially call you my boyfriend?"

I smile, we've never officially had a title before. "Yeah, Goldie, shits real this time." She smirks, and then places a chaste kiss to my lips before leaning back and forcing a groan from me when she shifts causing my cock to move inside her.

"Well, as my boyfriend, I order you to make your girl-friend a grilled cheese, put a movie on in the lounge and then eat me out under the blanket." I choke on fucking air. She shoots me a wink as she slides off me and walks her naked ass into the bathroom.

Her wish was my command. I sit on one end of the sofa with her feet on my lap while she lays back watching *Wednesday* and eats her grilled cheese. I never thought I would ever see my weekend spent like this, not with her and especially not with Corvin in the same house. I hear someone coming down the stairs and lean my head back to see Katie and her duo. She's wearing one of their shirts, her blonde hair is a fucking mess.

"Well fucked?" I ask the moment they spot us on the couch. Saint and Crue laugh, high fiving each other over Katie's head. Katie just turns a bright shade of red and ducks her head. Leah sits up and peers over the back of the sofa.

"Bitch, get your ass over here and spill the deets." I squeeze the shit out of her ankle.

"Ouch!" she yelps as she shoots me a dirty look.

"Sitting right fucking here!" I growl. She rolls her eyes.

"And you guys don't sit around talking about our asses and tits?" she sass's.

"No."

"Fuck no!"

"Nope," Saint, Crue and I all reply in unison, her jaw slackens as she looks from me to them.

"Seriously?" Katie asks.

Crue nods. "No guy wants another guy to know what his girl looks like naked. Would you want another girl knowing what mine and Saint's dicks looked like?"

"Oh shit," Leah breathes out, garnering the three of their attention. She smiles at her friend who looks distraught which confuses the fuck out of me.

"Not a freaking word!" Katie warns. Leah laughs and pretends to zip her lips and throw away the key.

"What the fuck was that?" Saint asks. I shrug as I look to Leah who looks like she is about to burst if she doesn't spit whatever it is out.

"Don't do it," Katie says in a stern voice, now I have to know. I run my hand up my girl's legs suggestively.

"I'll make you come." Four little words and she spills the beans just like I knew she would.

"Fine! That was the first time one of them has admitted that they're *all* sleeping together," she says it all so fast she's breathless and gasping for air.

"Uh, babe, everyone knew they were," I say.

She rolls her eyes. "Men, it's not official until it's said aloud, duh." The sound of a door opening upstairs draws all our attention to Corvin and Cody making their way downstairs. Corv is wearing a pair of shorts and Cody is in one of his shirts, red faced and smirking. They just fucked for sure. "That's nasty," Leah says the second she spots her brother. He shoots her a glare.

"I can't even look at you," he says in disgust, forcing me to turn away so he can't see my smile.

"Uh, why?" she asks, genuinely confused.

"Seriously?" Corvin snaps as he makes his way toward the other sofa with the rest of the crew following him. Cody drops down beside him while Saint, Crue and Katie take the bean bags. Leah looks to me. I take pity on my girl and lean over toward her to whisper.

"You were screaming my name loud enough for the neighbors to hear." I expect her to blush, cover her face or run from the room but what I don't expect is for her to laugh and point at her brother.

"Payback, fucker," she says through her laughter, which just causes everyone but Corvin to laugh along with her.

"Next ball I throw is aimed right at your dick, asshole," he spits at me, causing us all to laugh harder. Fuck, this feels good to be able to laugh with him and have no secrets between us. We all settle into comfortable silence as we watch the stupid show the girls all seem to enjoy. Beck comes ambling into the room halfway through the first episode. Leah sits up and pats the spot beside her. He drops down, smiling at her. She switches around so her feet are on his lap and her head rests on mine.

Good call, baby, I think to myself. If her head had of been on his lap, I would have smacked her ass right here in front of everyone. By the time the third episode rolls around, Leah is fast asleep and Cody is crashed out, snuggled into Corvin's side. I look down at the three on the floor and see Katie sleeping in Saint's arms while holding Crue's hand.

"I kind of feel bad," Corvin says to no one in particular.

"About what?" Crue asks.

"Beck's the only one not getting any action." I snort out a laugh and try to mask it by coughing. "I mean, Nathan is asleep upstairs," Corvin tacks on, earning a dry stare from Beck.

"Don't worry about me. I'm still sated from my recent action with Darius and a certain someone." The smile drops straight off Corvin's face, I'll admit I have to fight to keep from laughing because Beck just bummed Corvin right the fuck out.

"Dick move, asshole," Corv mutters. Saint grabs the remote and switches the channel. The rest of us mutter our thanks. The only reason I watch that shit is because of Leah.

Saint pauses his channel surfing when we spot a picture of Garrett being displayed on the news.

"Turn it up," Beck orders.

'Local homicide case has now been closed. Police have arrested the culprit who will be remanded in custody awaiting trial early next week. Garrett Jones family have said they don't understand how this could have happened, their son was loved and adored amongst his peers.' All of us mutter about how full of shit they are. Garrett wasn't liked by anyone. *'It's shocked the entire community to find out–'* The reporter stops speaking and presses on the earpiece in her ear, her eyes widen a second before she faces the camera again. *'I've just been notified of the identity of the alleged suspect.'* My eyes pop open so wide that they begin to water when a picture of Victor is plastered on the screen. *'Business mogul, Victor Hayes is now in police custody. Casey is live outside the station, over to you Casey.'*

Another woman appears on camera out in front of the local police station where we can see Victor in handcuffs being led inside by four officers. *'Yes, Maddie. I'm here as offi-cers lead Victor Hayes inside to process him. We have been informed that an eyewitness came forward with video evidence of Mr. Hayes at the site where Garrett Jones's remains were located. Police also found other evidence linking Mr. Hayes to the murder–'*

Saint puts the TV on mute, cutting off whatever else the reporter had to say. I sit here staring at the TV but not really seeing anything as my mind reels with what I just learned. Victor is going to jail for Garrett's murder. Victor was nowhere near that frat house last week.

"Darius!" I shake my head and turn to Corvin who looks slightly concerned. "You good?" I don't know how the hell I'm supposed to answer that. Do I care that he's in jail? I think about that for a second… No, I don't care what happens to that piece of shit but how the hell did he get convicted?

"Say something," Saint urges me.

"I don't know what to say," I utter quietly. I can feel all

their gazes on me and something inside me says there is one person responsible for this. Slowly I turn to face Beckett, who has a blank stare plastered on his face. "How?"

"This would be the part where I tell you that you have plausible deniability and would recommend that you are better off not knowing the details. All you need to know is he won't be getting out, nothing leads back to us and we're all in the clear to carry on living our lives." I see Beckett in a whole new light. We may not know everything about him or his past but he's proven time and time again that he's got all our backs. I nod before turning back to Corvin. I know the truth but I just need to hear him say it.

"He wasn't dead when you got back there, was he?" Corv cuts a glance to Saint and Crue before looking back to me.

"It makes no difference. Leah's safe and we have nothing to worry about, like Beck said. We never mention it again or ever speak about it. We leave it in the past and move on."

CHAPTER TWENTY-FIVE

Three weeks later…

It's the last day of school before Christmas break. I'm so ready to get the hell out of here and spend the next two weeks at the cabin with my *boyfriend*–I don't think I'll ever get tired of saying that word. Corv and the others are coming too, even Nathan and my girls. I managed to convince Val and Dawson to come along as well. We met up the day I started back to school and stopped doing online classes. She is fucking awesome and so is her son. Dawson is the sweetest little boy you will ever meet. When I went over to their apartment that's off campus, my heart broke. It's a tiny one-bedroom apartment, not in the best area but she wasn't granted a twin suite in the dorm and couldn't afford to pay to live on campus whilst being a mom and student. I girl tutors and cleans just to make enough money to cover their living expenses. When I found out they would be alone for Christmas, I practically forced her to come with us. Her and Dawson are riding up with me, Cody and Katie.

"Ready, bitches?" Cody shouts as I finish packing the last

of my stuff. I zip up my duffle and shoot her a toothy grin as I nod.

"Let's go!" I squeal as I make my way out of mine and Darius's room. Yeah, so, he got his way and I moved in here with him. The girls moved back into our old dorm room. Corvin had paid for my dorm for the year, so Katie jumped at the chance to share with Cody instead of going back to her old room. Honestly, I'm happy for them because I love coming home every day and getting to cuddle up with my *boyfriend*. Fuck, it's only been like six hours and I miss him already.

"Come on, bitches," Katie shouts the moment we come out the front door. I lock it before running over to Cody's car. I dump my bag in the trunk before calling shotgun and slipping in next to Cody, forcing Katie to sit in the back. I rattle off the directions to Val's place and Cody plugs it into her GPS. Fifteen minutes later we pull up out the front of Val's place. She's standing on the sidewalk with Dawson beside her. Cody parks and I jump out to help load her bags as she straps Dawson's car seat into the car. She makes it look easy as hell putting that thing in. She buckles Dawson into his seat, then she rounds the car and hops in the middle seat.

"Let's roll!" I shout excitedly, it's an eight hour drive to the cabin so we won't get there until late tonight but none of us care, we all just want to get the hell out of here. My phone rings, the girls groan knowing who it is since he decided to change his ringtone to *our* song. I pull it out of my pocket and hit answer.

"Hey, you." I ignore Cody fake gagging beside me.

"Hey, baby, have you left yet?" God just the sound of his voice has me practically panting.

"Yeah, we're just hitting the interstate now." The guys left last night to get everything set up and to do the food shopping for us. The girls and I couldn't leave until today because the three of us and even Val had papers due and we couldn't miss it.

"Thank fuck, we are never fighting again." I frown.

"Uh, we're not fighting," I tell him.

"Well if we do fight, we are never sleeping apart again. I fucking hated rolling over and not having you next to me." My heart fucking bursts inside my chest.

"Agreed. I hated not waking up next to you," I whine like a petulant toddler.

"I make ew better, Lee," Dawson calls out from the back. I peer around my seat and shoot the little guy a wink.

"Shit, I forgot about the kid. No screaming for you then," Darius quips. I laugh, unable to keep it in.

"There will be none of that!" I hear Corvin shouting in the background.

"I better go before he starts getting big mad," I tease.

"Okay, baby, drive safe and I'll see you tonight, beautiful."

"Love you."

"Love you too, Goldie." I'll never tire of hearing him say those words to me. I end the call smiling, while excitement thrums through me. I never thought Darius and I would ever find our way back to each other. We have gone through some tough shit but I believe it has made us stronger. He continues to tell me daily how much he loves me and promises to never hurt me again. I believe him and tell him that, except each night he says he has to show my body he means it. If this is what I get for the rest of my life, I won't be mad about it. I'll drop to my knees and thank G.O.D himself.

"You two are so cute it makes me sick," Cody mocks.

"And seeing you and my brother together doesn't make me ill?" I jibe, causing her to shake her head and shrug.

"We're just… hanging out." The longing in her voice has me feeling sorry for her. Corvin won't commit to her and I have no idea why. Cody is amazing and I can tell she really does care about my brother, but she is constantly getting hurt by him. She won't tell me what he does to make her cry, but the girl also can't seem to stay away from him.

"Are you sure everyone doesn't mind spending the holidays with a random girl and her kid?" Val asks shyly.

"Of course not," Katie reprimands.

"They'll love it. Nathan is excited to finally get to meet you and Dawson," I say. "Plus, it will finally stop Darius from thinking I made you up."

"Why would he think you made me up?" Val asks, confused.

"Darius is jealous of the toilet paper for touching her hoo-ha," Cody mocks, earning an eye roll from me.

"What's hoo-ha, Mommy?" Dawson asks. I cringe and shoot Val and apologetic look that she just waves off.

"Nothing, sweetie," she says as she places a kiss to his head. We spend the next few hours listening to music and singing along until Dawson falls asleep. Not wanting to wake the wee man, we cut the music and fill the car with conversation. Val asks about me and Darius. I tell her our story which has her swooning and claiming that we have an epic love story. Katie and Cody fill her in on their friendly relationships with Crue, Saint and Corvin.

"What about you?" I ask Val. She sighs and looks over at her son with a sad smile on her face.

"There isn't much to tell. I was sixteen and thought I was in love. He left, I found out eight weeks later I was pregnant. I tried to find him, even went to his house only to find it vacant. He disappeared from my life and broke my heart."

"I'm so sorry," I say quietly, feeling sorry for her. Darius ghosting me hurt but I can't imagine how hard that would have been if I was pregnant like Val.

"It's okay. I mean, he may have vanished but he left me behind the best gift I could have ever asked for. Dawson makes all the heartache worth it. I wouldn't change a thing." How she can be so upbeat and positive given her circumstances is admirable. I don't think I would be as strong as her if our roles were reversed. Being a single parent must be so tough, that thought has me thinking about Jenny Lockhart. Darius refuses to seek her out. He says he isn't ready and I respect that. I just hope one day he changes his mind and actually speaks to her so he can get the closure he needs from her.

He's had so much on his plate lately. He's busting his ass to train for football, studying, and learning the role of CFO of Saint Hart Holdings. He has now refused to go to Chicago, saying that he wants to go with Beck to Alaska. He's done that for me. He knows that I loved it there and said he would run shit from there and he and Beck would both learn the ropes of the resort and the daily running of the company. He and Beck both have been up late most nights working, their dedication awe inspiring. Darius leaves with Beck after the New Year—he's been asking me every day to go with him. I haven't decided what I want to do yet. After spending one night without him, I know there is no way I can go six months without seeing him every day. I grab my phone from the cup holder and text him.

> You win! Book me on that flight, baby, I'm coming with you Xx

I cringe when I think of having to switch back to online classes, again. I think if the guys weren't on the board I would have been kicked out already for fucking the administration around so much. My phone pings with his reply almost immediately.

BIG D

> Don't play with me, Goldie.

I'm not. Last night made me realize I can't be without you. I know you have to do this for your business.

BIG D

Our business, baby. Are you sure?

I've never been surer in my life.

BIG D

I fucking love you. I'll show you just how much this means to me when you get here.

I clench my thighs together to try to dull the ache that is beginning to form. I'm so far gone where he is concerned.

I expect you to show me all night long <3

We finally pull into the drive of the cabin just before eleven. We're all tired and sore from sitting in the car for so long. We only stopped once to use the restrooms and get food, refusing to stop again, too eager to get here. I spot Beck, Saint and Corv's cars parked in front of the garage and smile when I see Darius's bike there as well. Why they all didn't just come in two cars I have no idea. Nathan came with Saint. I love that he has slotted into our crazy family, he hangs with the guys just as much as us now.

"Oh my God," Val breathes from the backseat.

"Right? It's so beautiful here. Just wait till the morning when you get to see the view, it is gorgeous," Katie says. Cody parks the car and the four of us all jump out to stretch. God my ass is numb. I hear the front door open and squeal as I take off. I race down the pathway, smiling at the sight of my man running at me. I launch myself at him, clinging to him like a monkey and kiss the shit out of him. He grips my ass to keep me from slipping.

"Fuck, stop that!" I pull away and look over his shoulder to see my brother standing there with a sour look on his face. Darius places a quick kiss to the side of my neck before putting me back on my feet.

"Come on, let's grab your things." He grabs my hand and walks me back to the car. I introduce him and Corvin to Val. He seems at ease seeing for himself that she is actually a girl. He and Corvin carry Val's belongings while we grab the rest so she only has to worry about carrying a sleeping Dawson inside.

"Where's the guys?' Cody asks as we follow the guys inside.

"They tried to wait up but they crashed. Katie your boys said to tell you to lock the basement door after yourself." Katie rolls her lips over her teeth and nods. I freaking love how shy she gets, like the girl can take two dicks but as soon as you mention it out loud, she blushes. "Nathan took the fold out bed in the theater room, so, Val, you and your boy can have the spare room next to Darius's." I dart in front of the guys and open the door for them, the only light that is on is in the entryway. Truthfully, I'm beat and I think the others are as well, so Val will just have to wait till morning to get a tour of the cabin. Corvin pauses in the entryway and hands Katie her things. She's blushing so hard as she shoots us a quick wave and scurries off toward the basement. I attempt to move around Corvin and head upstairs, but he blocks my path. I look up at him and frown.

"What's up?" I ask. He smiles proudly and it throws me for a loop.

"I know shit has been hard for you but I just wanted to say I am so fucking proud of you for finishing you English paper and not quitting." I melt. "Also, Darius told me about Alaska." My shoulders tense thinking he's about to fight me on my decision. "I spoke with Mom and Dad and told them about it. They agree with me that this would be good for you."

"W-what?" I mumble, stunned as hell that he is being so... good about this.

He smiles down at me. "I may not enjoy the sight of you and dickhead together." Darius snorts beside me but Corv carries on. "But I also know he is a lot of the reason why you are doing so well. I expect your ass on a plane back to CHU to visit me every two months." I squeal and jump at him. He drops the bags to catch me. I hold him tight and love that my big brother is happy for me.

"I love you, Corv," I whisper, feeling him soften against me.

"I love you to, Lee."

CHAPTER TWENTY-SIX

Darius

I place Val and her kid's bag in the spare room while Leah helps her settle in and tells her where the bathroom is. Val thanks her and tells her that she'll see her in the morning. Leah promises to give her a tour and introduce her to everyone then. I'm beginning to grow impatient as I wait for her. My cock is rock fucking hard and dying to be buried balls deep inside my girl. I mean, I did promise to show her how much I loved her *all* night long. I never break a promise.

"Leah, go, I swear we will be fine." Leah nibbles on her bottom lip and nods.

"Okay, if you need me I'm right next door," she says before heading my way. I close Val's door after Leah, place my hand on the small of her back and practically push her into our room. She stumbles forward a step and spins to face me as I close our bedroom door. "What the heck?" she whisper-shouts.

"Strip." Her eyes widen at my demand.

"What?" I quirk a brow, daring her to defy me again as I say,

"Either you strip willingly or I rip them off, but either way, Goldie, I'm getting inside that pussy." Her eyes flare to life with lust, a small smirk breaking free as she unzips her jacket and lets it drop to the floor. Her top is next to go, then lastly is her jeans. She stands there in nothing but a purple bra and thong that has my mouth watering, needing to taste her.

"Come get me," she says in a sultry tone that has my cock twitching in my sweats. I eliminate the space between us, grip the back of her neck and haul her up toward my face, forcing her to stand on her tiptoes. She grips my shirt in her dainty little hands, her breaths coming in quick pants.

"You wet for me, Goldie?" I ask as I brush my cheek along hers, loving how a shiver shoots through her at the feeling of my stubble against her skin. I nibble on her lobe, loving the small whimper that escapes her. I dart my tongue out and lick her ear relishing in the shudder that overcomes her. Fuck, I love how reactive she is to my touch. "It's been over twenty-four hours since I've been inside this pussy, baby, I think I need to remedy that." I grip her waist and lift her, like always she locks her legs around my waist. She peers down at me with raw hunger in her gaze as I walk us back toward the bed. "I never got to fuck you last time in here, so we need to ruin every surface of this room with your cum."

"Fuck, yes," she breathes out. I fall forward crushing her beneath my weight against the mattress. I grind my cock into her and crash my lips against hers, at the same time swallowing her moan of pleasure. I continue to do that until she is a writhing mess of need beneath me, only then do I pull back and slip off the bed. I look down at her, red faced and panting. Her eyes beg me to fuck her until she is nothing but putty in my arms. I run my gaze down her flushed body. A satisfied smirk makes its way onto my face when I see the wet patch in the middle of her thong.

"You dirty little girl." She squirms as I reach down and peel the scrap of lace down her toned legs, bring it to my nose and inhale her heady scent. Her mouth drops open in surprise, and before she can utter a word I ball up the lace and shove it inside her mouth, causing her eyes to widen. "Can't have you screaming and waking up your friend's kid now, can we?" She shakes her head and tries to clench her thighs together. I grip her knees and push them wider. "You close these again and I'll make sure you don't come for hours." Her eyes widen to the size of dinner plates. I grip the back of my shirt and pull it over my head, her greedy gaze roams over my exposed skin and slowly lowers to my sweats, expecting them to go next.

Silly girl, I plan to draw this out and make her fucking beg for my cock before finally giving it to her. I yank the cups of her bra down and suck her nipple into my mouth. She arches her back off the bed, the thong in her mouth muffles her cries. I glide my teeth along her hardened peak before swiping my tongue over it. I pay the other side the same amount of attention before I lick a trail down her body, stopping at her belly button and hiding my smile when she begins to groan out her annoyance. I slip off the edge of the bed, drop to my knees, grip her legs and yank her down until her pussy is directly in front of me.

I reach out and part her folds with my fingers, stifling my own groan when I see the slickness dripping out of her. I lean down and run my nose along the inside of her thigh, loving the whimpers that come from her. I keep doing this until she is shaking and only then do I take pity on her and swipe my tongue through her wet cunt. The second the taste of her arousal hits my tongue I moan, a need so strong and dominant overcomes me, forcing the need for me to make her come my soul purpose in this moment. I push my tongue inside her tight wet hole. She bucks her hips. I place my hand flat against her stomach holding her in place as I eat what is mine. I push my tongue in out of her before replacing my tongue with two fingers and sucking her clit into my mouth.

"Hmmmm," she cries out, writhing beneath me. I pump in and out of her, keeping a steady pace as I alternate between sucking and licking her clit. I can feel her tense and know she won't last much longer so I slow my pace—orgasm denial is torture but when I do eventually allow her to come, it will be the most intense orgasm of her life. I do this three more times, bringing her right to the cusp of climax before stopping. She grips a handful of my hair and yanks it hard, telling me she's about to go crazy. I peek up at her reddened face and smile.

"Want to come, baby?" She lifts her head, narrows her eyes at me and tries to hurl what I'm sure are a few choice words, but thanks to the lace in her mouth, I don't hear shit. It's the look in her green eyes that tells me if I deny her again she is going to rip my cock off. That's all it takes for me to stand and finally push my sweats and boxers down my legs, exposing my cock. It's angry and hard as stone from being teased by the taste of her. I push her legs wider to accommodate me, lifting them and resting her ankles against my shoulders, then pushing on the backs of her thighs to push her knees against her chest. Lining my cock up, I slowly slide inside her. The feeling of being inside her is like none other. Her eyes roll back as her mouth opens but her thong masks the sounds. When I'm halfway inside her, I pause for a second before slamming all the way, loving the muffled scream that tears from her throat.

I push forward until her ankles are either side of her head and shift up into an almost standing position. She reaches out and grips the sides of my arms, needing something to hold onto. I pull almost all the way out before slamming inside her, keeping a quick and steady pace, knowing how she loves to be fucked hard. Leah may look like a goody two shoes in the street but my girl is a freak in the sheets! Her nails dig into the sides of my arms, her body becomes taut, ready for her impending orgasm to rip through her. The sounds coming from her grow in pitch the closer she gets to her release. I place my hand over her mouth to keep her quiet. I slam inside her harder and deeper making sure to hit that sweet spot. Leah's eyes roll back, her back arches off the bed.

"Come for me, Goldie." As if my words are her undoing she comes all over my cock, her screams muted by my hand. I can't bring her down slowly, the need to mark her and make sure everyone knows who she belongs to consumes me. I lurch back pulling out of her. Gripping my cock in my hand, I pump it three times watching as jets of my cum spurt all over her stomach and tits, her name tearing from deep inside me. My chest rises and falls in rapid succession as I stare down at her all flushed and eyes dazed. I reach down and smear my cum all over her. Call me possessive or whatever the fuck you like, but knowing that my cum is all over her, marking her as mine, has me wanting to beat my fists against my chest.

I slowly blink my eyes and yawn. Leah was insatiable last night. We barely slept, needing to be connected and reminding the other who we belong to. I flick my gaze around the room and bite my lip to stop my laugh from breaking free. We fucked everywhere and the destruction all over my room shows that. I roll over and bury my face in the crook of her neck. She moans as I wrap my arm around her waist and pull her naked body flush against my chest.

"Hmmm, I need more sleep," she mutters with sleep thick in her tone. I smile into her neck.

"I'm hungry," I whisper huskily, a shiver rolls through her at my double meaning.

"Is everyone awake?"

"Hell if I know, why?" She rolls over and smiles at me. Fuck she looks so beautiful. Leah's beauty is something I can't even put into words, the sight of her steals my breath away. I reach out and cup her cheek as I lean in and kiss her. Touching her, kissing her or even fucking her isn't a want, it's a *need*. I can't be without her. When I ghosted her for two years, I was half a man, lost and spiraling. I didn't know why I couldn't find happiness or a reason to be grateful for what I had achieved in life until she came back. The world seemed better, colors looked brighter and food tasted richer. Leah is my reason, my purpose for everything in life and I'll never lose sight of that again.

She pulls back, smiling at me with love in her eyes. "I would love to stay here with you all day but I need to be there for Val and introduce her to everyone." I sigh in annoyance.

"Did you have to bring her?" I grumble.

She swats me on the chest. "Babe, she would have been alone for Christmas. I couldn't do that to her and Dawson." As much I hate to admit it, I love that she cares about everyone and always goes above and beyond for those she loves. Just sometimes I wished she was selfish like me, so she wouldn't feel guilty about spending the day in bed, fucking me.

"Doesn't she have family?" Leah's brows draw in as she shakes her head.

"I don't think so. She hasn't said anything but she did say she's been on her own since she was pregnant with Dawson." Sadness is thick in her tone.

"Where's the kid's dad?"

"He took off before Val could tell him she was pregnant." What a fucking drop kick. Who the fuck does that? Man, I could never turn my back on Leah if she was pregnant. I don't want kids anytime soon because I can't stand the thought of sharing her with anyone, even our own kid.

"Fine. You have an hour to eat and hang out with your friend, then we're hitting the hot tub so I can fuck your ass while your pussy is being destroyed by the jets." The sadness in her eyes for her friend is gone, replaced by raw hunger for *me*. Fuck, I'll never tire of seeing that look in her eyes.

"I love you." I smile triumphantly knowing I'll be the only

man in this world to ever hear those words come from her sinful lips.

"I love you too, Goldie. Now, get the fuck outta the bed or I'll be balls deep inside you in a second flat and your friend can face the crew by herself."

CHAPTER TWENTY-SEVEN

Leah

You best believe I leapt out of that bed like it was on fire, Darius would have kept his word and pinned me down until I was screaming his name. I managed to snag the shower before Val. Of course, I only managed to have mere minutes alone before Darius stormed in, demanding that I help him deal with a situation. The situation of course was me helping get rid of his boner, which did lead to me plastered against the shower, biting down on his shoulder so my screams didn't wake the whole house. When we finally exited the shower after using all the hot water, I quickly brushed my teeth and combed my hair before changing.

I'm sitting on the end of our bed pulling on my Ugg boots when a knock sounds at the door. Darius pulls his hoodie on before going to open it. The bedroom door opens to reveal a sleepy Val with a smiling Dawson in her arms. I pull my boot on and stand, making way over to them to pluck Dawson from her hold and kissing his gorgeous face until he is laughing and begging me to stop.

"Could I ask a favor?" I see Darius stiffen next to me but I ignore as I look at my friend.

"Of course, Val. What do you need?" She seems nervous.

"Could you please watch him while I take a quick shower. I swear I won't be long. I'm just worried about the stairs if he came out of the room while I was in there and—" I cut her off, feeling so sad for her that she feels like asking to watch her son for five minutes is a huge burden.

"Val!" She clamps her mouth closed and pales slightly. I try to smile reassuringly to help ease some of her nerves. "Go shower, wash your hair, do whatever you want and take your time. Darius and I will take Dawson down and get him breakfast. Crue and Saint will love having the little guy to play with." Her eyes widen.

"Are you sure?" I shift Dawson to one side and use my free hand to rest against Val's shoulder in a comforting gesture.

"Yes! Go shower, take your time. When you're done, breakfast will be ready and waiting for you downstairs." Her eyes grow misty.

"Thank you, Leah." Her tone is watery and that fucking hurts me.

"Val, we're all here for you. Once you get to know the guys, you will understand that we are family and we take care of our own. You and Dawson are ours now. Whatever you need, we got you." She swallows loudly as her eyes fill with tears. Before they can fall, she nods and scurries back to her room. I turn to Darius to find him staring at the spot Val just vacated with a look of pain etched into his beautiful face. "Are you okay?" He shakes his head and nods.

"Yeah. Come on, let's go eat." I hate that I know he is lying, it's hard for him to see a mom care for her child. I hope one day my man can find it within himself to find his mom and speak with her because I hate that there is this hurt inside him that I can't take away.

🏈

I smile as I look around the table at everyone. Dawson sits on my lap eating the pancakes Beck made him. Beck and Darius sit on either side of us. Nathan, Corv, Crue, Cody, Katie and Saint all shout and laugh as they fight over who can beat who at Mario Kart. I shake my head and hide my smile as I place a kiss to the top of Dawson's head.

"I go Becky?" Silent laughter shakes my shoulder as I hear Beck grunt beside me. When we came down this morning to see everyone and get some food, I introduced Dawson to the others and I may have forgotten to introduce Beck as *Beck* and not Becky. Dawson instantly took a shine to Beck and demanded to stay with him and help make pancakes. I was stunned when Beck plucked him from my arms and set him up on the counter to help. Dawson reaches out for Beck, the big man's eyes soften as he grabs Dawson from me and sits him on his lap, wrapping his arms around him protectively. Darius drapes his arm around my shoulder as I stare at the duo beside me. He leans in and whispers, low enough for only me to hear.

"Stop looking at my best friend like that." There's heat in his tone that has me turning to face him, we're so close that our noses brush against each other.

"Huh?" His eyes narrow but he can't hide the lust that sparks to life in those beautiful eyes.

"Keep looking at him like that and I may have to make a mini me just so you'll look at me like that." My eyes snap wide, he laughs before pecking me on the lips and leaning back in his chair while I stare at him.

"Get the hell away from my son!" I snap my gaze to the dinning entry way to see Val standing there with an angry look on her face. The room is doused in silence from her outburst.

"Valance..." Beck whispers beside me. I flick my gaze between her and him as he slowly stands from his chair with Dawson still in his hold. The moment he steps away from the table she rushes toward them stopping a foot away from Beck.

"Give him to me now!" she grits out, her tone is hard but I can hear the hurt that she tries to mask. They know each other, how? Beck looks down at the boy in his arms before turning back to Val—Valance. I thought Val was short for Valerie or something, I never thought to ask her.

"He's your… son?" Beck clips out. Val's eyes widen for a split second. I slowly stand from my chair and move to stand beside Beck.

"Yes," she grits out, her features pull taut. She darts her gaze to me, pleading for my help silently.

"Becky, pass me Dawson," I say but Beck ignores me as he keeps his gaze on Val.

"How old is he, Valance?" His tone is laced with anger. Val's shoulders bunch, her hands clench into fists at her sides as she holds his angry stare.

"He's… four." Beckett's brows jump to his hairline as his eyes widen, Dawson reaches for his mother. Val lurches forward and yanks him from Beckett's hold, clutching her son against her chest as she peppers kisses on his head. She darts her gaze to me, this time all I see in her eyes is regret and pain. "I need to go home." Those five words seem to have Beck snapping out of whatever trance he was in, he closes the space between him and Val, glaring down at her.

"You aren't taking *my* son anywhere!" he snarls, and gasps break out around the table. My jaw unhinges as I stare at the couple in front of me. Dawson is Beck's kid, how? Val's blue eyes burn with hatred as she scowls up at Beck.

"Fuck you, Beckett. He isn't yours!" A humorless laugh leaves Beck, the sound of it has me tensing knowing something bad is coming.

"He isn't mine?" Val nods stiffly. "Right, so, Valance, why the fuck did you name *your* son after me?" I frown unsure what he means. Val shakes her head.

"Oh shit." I snap my gaze to Darius as he stares at Beck's back. "Beckett Dawson." Oh fuck!

"Please, don't," Val chokes out, drawing my attention back to them.

"You gave *my* son my last name as his first name," Beck shouts. Dawson cries in fright, Val tries to soothe him but he continues to cry. "You're not taking him anywhere!"

"Screw you, Beckett. You'll never get near him again," Val says with so much conviction I actually believe her.

"I'll take your ass to court. I have the money and you don't, so say your goodbyes now." Val's face pales, panic fills her features for a second before she hardens her gaze before taking a deep breath.

"Take me to court and I'll tell them how you are a murderer. You and I both know I have the proof of your crime." The icy tone of her voice fills me with dread. I feel Darius behind me as he wraps his arms around my waist and pulls me flush against his chest. The guys stand from their seats with angry glares pointed directly at Val, who looks like a deer caught in the headlights.

"You can try, but heed my warning, *Valance*," Darius spits her name like it burns his tongue. "You run your mouth to anyone and I promise you that we will bury you six feet fucking deep and take that kid from you without remorse." Tears flow down her cheeks, she darts her gaze to me for help but I'm stuck. She's my friend but Beck is... my Becky. He's one of my ride or dies and I can't turn my back on him. Which is why, when Beck yanks Dawson from her arms I don't intervene, not even when Crue and Corvin grip her arms pulling her from the room.

Thank you!

Holy shit, honest to G.O.D I never expected these books to go the way they did but fuck I'm not even mad about it! Darius and Leah are the best fucking thing since sliced bread, I can't even tell you how much I love these two!

Well, obviously thanks to that ending you know Becky is getting a book, duh! After that scene with him and Darius fucking Leah and how close he got to her I just knew he needed a book. I freaking hope you loved Darius and Leah as much as I do because I just may cry if you don't! I love how much of a bad bitch Leah is and refuses to cower away from Darius even when he is dick.

Thank you for taking a chance and reading *Offside* and *Touchdown*, these books hold a special place in my heart. I never thought I could ever pull off writing a sports romance let alone make it a bully but voila! Here we are and I couldn't be more grateful.

If you could leave a review on Amazon, Bookbub or Goodreads that would be freaking amazing!

THANK YOU!

Beck's book be out shortly so keep an eye out for the pre-
order of his book, *Endgame*.

Ruined By The Rook

<u>**Fairytales With A Twist**</u>

Condemned Beast

SPORTS ROMANCE

<u>**Playing For Keeps**</u>

<u>**Duet**</u>

Offside

Touchdown

End Game

Hail Mary

RH SPORTS

Hate Us Like You Mean It

Acknowledgments

Marcus, obviously had to put you in here because I need to thank you for allowing me to use your juicy dick as inspo for the sex scenes in these books! I'm still fucking salty you wouldn't let me bring another guy into the room to try out the three-way you party pooper, you're lucky you have an amazing dick or I would be rioting for you declining me about a threesome!

Leah, these books wouldn't be here without you babe so I can't thank you enough for allowing me to share your story! I'm so glad you never shot your shot or I wouldn't have been able to write these books xxx

Tash, Clare, and Sarah, my Beta/Alpha girls. I couldn't do this without you ladies so thank you from the bottom of my heart for pushing to always write daily and telling me when a bit in the book is shit lol I love you!

My ARC team, fuck you ladies are the light of my life man, I can't even put into words what you ladies mean to me. I never thought I would find a group that I could fit in with and yet here we are, you ladies are fucking amazing, and thank you for loving each of these and the characters as much as I do.

Lizz, oh my God, thank you so fucking much for everything you have done on these books! You make them all perfect and pretty and I can't thank you enough, I freaking love you.

My babies, thank you for being you and allowing me to hide away and work nonstop so I can get these books out. You are

both my driving force and I love you more than words can
express. Xxx
Last but not least, my amazing readers,
Thank you from the bottom of my cold dead-ass heart for
loving all these books and taking a chance on me. Your
support and love is the reason why I get to live out my dream
of being an author, I appreciate each and every one of you.
I love you.

Sam
Xxxx

About the Author

Samantha Barrett is a dark romance, PNR author who loves to write out-of-the-box stories. She is originally from the land of the long white cloud, New Zealand. She is totally fluking her way through this whole author gig, if she isn't writing you can find her kicking back with her kids and husband with a bag of chips and a glass of wine in her hand.
Sam loves Twilight and is a TWIHARD proudly.